In Virginia's Shoes

Linda Becker

Seeker Publishing

ISBN 978-0-578-05775-0

Cover design, graphics and photography by
Linda Becker

*This work of fiction is lovingly
dedicated to my grandma, Virginia Rose,
whose life and spirit inspired me
to create this book.*

Chapter 1

They were tiny—barely 3 inches long—and pink. A delicate pink fabric over a soft sole and embroidery of flowers was on the toes. Little shell buttons held the fragile straps across my feet. Do I remember wearing them? No. But I remember looking at them when I was older. My mother saved them for me. I gave them to my daughter, who displays them in an old trunk along with some other "antique" items that used to belong to me. More fragile now than when they were new—just like me—those tiny pink shoes were my first.

"Mom? Mom? Can you hear me? Do you know where you are?" It was my daughter's voice speaking to me, pulling me out of my dream state. I could hear her, but I couldn't see her. My eyelids were so heavy. My head felt dizzy. Slowly I pried my eyelids open and blinked away the fuzziness to see my daughter and granddaughter standing in front of my bed. But this wasn't my bed. It was a hospital bed in the middle of a hospital room. I carefully turned my head from side to side to take in my surroundings. The room was large. Everything in it seemed to be white from the white blinds on the windows to the white laminate cabinets that lined the white walls. It was as if someone had tragically drained my world of all color. The only warmth in the room that I could see was in these two people standing in front of me waiting for me to answer.

"Mom, can you hear me? How are you feeling?" asked this 60 year old woman who was my only daughter, Eleanor.

My granddaughter, Lisa, stood next to her mother. She was Eleanor's second child of three. Lisa was already a grown woman with a child of her own. I was 96 years old. I stared at them both wondering how time could have moved so quickly. I tried my best to answer them.

It was difficult to speak. My throat was dry and sore. My lips were also dry and tight. I couldn't seem to get them to form any words, so I nodded, as if to say I was feeling okay. I wondered why I woke up in this hospital room, but again, I couldn't speak. I looked at my daughter with questions in my eyes. *What am I doing here? Where am I? What happened?* I wanted so badly to say the words, but my mouth would not cooperate. I suppose it was obvious what I wanted to know, because she began to explain.

"Mom, do you remember falling last night?"

I wrinkled my brow to answer, "No".

"You fell last night at your house. You must have hit your head when you did, because they found you unconscious. Apparently you were awake long enough to push your alert button before you passed out. Thank God you had that button around your neck. It probably saved your life. If the ambulance hadn't gotten to you as fast as it did, I hate to think what might have happened to you. Mom, apparently you passed out on top of your floor register. The heat from it gave you third degree burns on your chest. Your skin was nearly burned off, and they needed to do some repair work on it. That's why they had to bring you to St. Louis by helicopter. You needed to be in a burn unit. Do you understand what I'm telling you?"

A burn unit? Helicopter? What was she talking about? I couldn't remember any of this. I'm terrified to fly. How did they get me in a helicopter? I wondered…

I couldn't remember anything. Or could I? I tried very hard to think back. I leaned my head back onto my pillow and my eyes blurred the multitude of white objects into a cloud as I tried to recall the night before.

I remember being awakened in the middle of the night by the phone ringing. I remember getting out of bed. I remember the cold hard wood floor under my bare feet. I closed my eyes and I could see it. Yes, I remembered the hard wood floor. It was winter and the floor was ice cold as my feet traveled across it. It was dark and I could barely see. I remember being awakened by a noise. Was it a phone ringing? What was it that awakened me? It wasn't a phone ringing. No, it was a voice, a familiar one. It was the sound of my mother's voice. I leaned back and I listened as my mother called me…

"Jenny! Wake up! Go outside and drain your whistle!" That was a familiar sound. Every morning my mother would wake me up the same way. She knew I had a tendency to wet the bed, so she woke me up first thing to go outside and take care of my business. I was 10 years old. My name was Virginia Sommers. I was named after the state in which I was born, but everyone called me Jenny.

I hesitantly pulled myself out from under heavy quilts of the bed I shared with my sister, Katie, and set my bare feet on the wood floor. Ooh! It was cold! But of course wood floors usually are cold on early November mornings before sunrise. I pulled on my black winter boots and wrapped myself up in my thick wool coat over my night gown and made my way to the outhouse.

Ouch! The bitter air hit my nose like cold steel, as I opened the door of our little rock house. My father built that little house himself for our family two years earlier, when he and my mother decided to make Southern Illinois our home. They'd traveled from Lynchburg, Virginia to Kentucky to Oklahoma and finally settled here just on the outskirts of what would one day be known as the Shawnee National Forest. Our house rested high on a hill overlooking the beautiful countryside and was surrounded by forestland, which gave it kind of a magical feeling to a ten year old girl. The forest of pines was a wonderful place to imagine that I was a princess hiding away in a little cottage, waiting for my prince to come rescue me.

I spent many summer days pretending just that. I would hide in the nearby woods from the imaginary evil queen. I heard a sound! Quickly I turned to see it was only a startled deer darting past. When I knew it was safe, I would wander out of the trees and up onto the hill. Past the pond and across a few rolling hills I could see my prince riding on his white horse making his way to find me!

This morning there was no time for imagining anything except maybe heat. I marched my way through the darkness as my boots crunched the frosted grass. The cold had already found its way through the boots and into my small bare feet hiding inside. At least there wasn't any snow, yet, to trudge through. I hated the cold! I hated that winter hadn't even fully come yet. The nights would still grow longer and the days shorter. I hated the dark and longed for the light.

With every footstep I cursed the winter and the cold! I longed for brighter spring mornings and the sound of birds chirping, telling me to get up and enjoy the day. I longed for a new awakening and the first hints of summer to come! I found myself dreaming of soft green grass under my feet. I tried desperately to imagine the warmth and shut out the chill that was my reality. With my business completed, I went back into the house and warmed myself by the coal stove. Soon enough, I thought, summer would be here and all would be right again.

Summer did come in the year of 1918, but not in its usual joyful way for me. My mother, Grace, died in June at the age of 27 while pregnant with her 5th child. I was now 11. My brother, Charles Lynn, was 9, and my sister, Katie, was 2. The baby died along with my mother. Back then we didn't really know what was wrong or how to fix it. They said my mother's blood pressure ran up so high that she had a stroke. It didn't really matter too much to me how she had died. I just knew I was now without a mother.

The funeral was held at Olive Baptist Church in Ozark, Illinois not far from where we lived. There were a lot of people packed into that little church—more than I think I'd ever seen in one place at the same time. I remember how hot it was with all those bodies pent up inside that tiny church. Drops of sweat fell from my forehead and joined my tears falling from my eyes.

We were singing, "Amazing Grace, how sweet the sound that saved a wretch like me…" I remembered how that song had always puzzled me. Since my mother's name was Grace and toward the end of the song it went something like, "'tis Grace has brought me safe thus far, and Grace will lead me home." When I was very little and I heard that song, I thought they were singing about my mother. I'd say, "Momma, are we singing about you? Are you going to lead us home?" She'd just smile and put her finger to her mouth for me to hush during church service and then go on singing. I was pretty sure the song was about her. I knew it also had something to do with God and Heaven. I knew my mom had something to do with Heaven too, so it all kind of made sense in my child's mind.

As we sang that lovely hymn at her funeral, those early memories came back to me and I was now sure that we must be singing about my mother. She had brought me safe this far and I knew she was in heaven waiting to bring me there someday. It made me happy to think of her welcoming me into heaven, but I wished she had waited a little longer to go. I needed her with me here still.

Zion Cemetery is located at a large bend in the Ozark Road. On one side of the road is the Old Zion Cemetery where you'll find graves dating back to the Civil War. On the other side of the road are a small brick church and the newer gravesites. The ground slopes down from the church into a small valley and then quickly comes back up to form a hill before it meets the road again. It was on that hill that my mother's body was buried next to my little brother, Curtis, who had died when he was 3 months old. The baby was buried next to her with a tiny headstone that simply read "Infant Son".

I'll never forget that sad summer afternoon, as I watched my father say goodbye to the woman he loved and his stillborn son. I think it was then that I realized how much he truly loved my mother. Sometimes you don't really notice something until it's no longer there. That is how it was with my father. There had been a light in him that was bright and happy, kind and caring and very much alive when my mother was around. Now that she was gone, the light had been snuffed out. I never saw it return. He rarely ever spoke about her and he never remarried.

Chapter 2

At the age of eleven I wore my mother's shoes, figuratively speaking. It was apparent after just a few months that fall, that I couldn't continue with school, raise 2 children and run a home. I left school—and my childhood—behind forever. I woke up before the sun and started a fire in the cook stove. I made biscuits and cooked a little bacon before waking my brother for school. I made his and my father's lunch, which usually consisted of some lard smeared on a biscuit, and sent them off to work and school. I spent my days doing laundry, mending, cooking, cleaning and watching over my little sister, Katie. I went to sleep after everyone else and awoke the next morning before they did to do it all over again.

Gone were my carefree days of walking the Hunting Branch Trail to my little one-room schoolhouse and playing with my friends. Gone were the days of playing with dolls and dreaming of being someone's bride. Dolls had been replaced with 2 real children who needed my mothering. Romantic dreams had no place in my head filled with lists of chores that must be done. There was really no time to be sad either. I was raised with good German work ethics and I was blessed with a strong spirit. We were country folk and we knew how to survive. We didn't dwell on hard times. We accepted the work that needed to be done and we did it.

I say there wasn't time to be sad, but there was a loneliness—an emptiness—that wasn't there before my mother's death. It is an unexplainable feeling when your mother is no longer there. Her absence leaves a hole that no one else can fill. I missed her strength. I missed being cared for and feeling secure. It was selfish, but I wanted so badly to feel her stroke my hair again and tell me that everything would be alright, like she had so many times before. Now, there was no one to look to for that reassurance. Somewhere deep in my heart I yearned for my mother's irreplaceable love for the rest of my life.

My days were well determined. My schedule rarely changed. I became accustomed to 3 people depending on me for nearly everything. It was that time in my life, I believe, that formed the person I would become. I learned to cook and to do it well. Clothes, towels and sheets were expensive, so I did my best to keep them clean, neat and in good mending. I found that I had a real talent for sewing and taught myself to cut patterns and sew new clothes for us. Eventually word got around of my skills and I was able to earn a little money by taking in others' mending and laundry. It was nice to have a little extra money around for necessities like shoes for the kids when they started back to school.

Time went by quickly. I was 11, then 12, then 16. I was a young woman, but I felt like I was 30. I think I looked like it also. I was never what anyone would call a beautiful little girl. My hair was light brown and long. I wore it braided most of the time to keep it neat. My features weren't pretty, but they were striking. I had my father's light blue eyes that were a good contrast to my brown hair and olive skin. They were deep set like my mother's eyes had been, and I had her heavy brow and strong cheek bones. Not the usual delicate traits of a young girl, but an unusual face that made me stand out from the rest.

Every day seemed pretty much like the day before, and it seemed like life would just always be like it was then. I couldn't imagine that anything would ever change. I really never wished that it would. It was a simple, comfortable life. I didn't think I would ever need or want or find anything more.

In the summer of 1923 I was able to take some time away from the family to visit my cousin Julie in the "big city" of Marion. I was 16 years old. I suppose I should have been thinking that my life was just beginning, but instead I had resigned myself to the idea that it had passed me by. I had been a housewife and mother of two for the last 5 years. Honestly I didn't know any other way to be.

Julie was my favorite cousin. She was always fun to be around, and I thought she was the most beautiful girl I'd ever seen. Her blonde curls formed a perfect frame for her perfect little doll face with bright blue eyes and pink cheeks. She looked just like a doll when she was a girl, and now that she was a young woman, she looked like the movie stars on the posters outside the theatre! Julie always had lovely clothes, too. And although she had so much, she was never conceited or boastful or bratty. She was just as sweet as could be, and I loved her.

Julie's father, my Uncle Frank, and his wife, Sarah, opened up a little store in town and had been very prosperous. Uncle Frank, Aunt Sarah, Julie, and her sister Viola lived above their store on Second Street. How I enjoyed visiting Julie and Viola when we were little girls! It had been years since I had been to town to visit. Julie, Viola and I were grown now and finding our way in the world as young women. I wondered if we would still find that same girlish fun now that we were older.

On this particular visit, a neighbor and his wife had graciously offered me a ride into town on their buggy. Although most people were driving cars in town, no one we knew had one out in the country. I thanked them for the lift as I stepped down onto the dirt road. The dust quickly covered my brown leather pumps until they appeared to be more of a light tan color. I did my best to brush the dust off of them when I reached the sidewalk.

I walked my dusty brown pumps down the sidewalk to Uncle Frank's store and walked inside. The sweet smell of tobacco and the bright colors of various striped candy sticks greeted me. Uncle Frank's store carried a variety of merchandise, from food items to clothing. The walls were lined with wooden shelves that held oats and cereals, tobacco, flour, and salt. In the middle of the store were bolts of beautiful fabrics—gingham checks, bright plaids, and rich-colored velvets. Past the fabrics were racks of ready-made clothes. They carried dresses, blouses, slacks, men's suits, and coveralls. There was even a little soda fountain in the back.

No one was at the front counter, so I walked through, brushing the soft cottons and velvets with my fingers as I did. Past the dresses and shirts and pants to the little soda fountain I went. A young man I'd never seen before was standing behind the counter—his face buried deep into a magazine. As he heard me approach, he raised his head to greet me. The most handsome face I ever saw looked up at me and said, "Hi, may I help you?"

I believe I said something like "Hello", but I was never quite sure, because I was so taken by his devastating good looks. He simply took my breath away. I somehow regained some composure to bring the words out of my mouth to explain who I was. He spoke again, but I couldn't hear a thing he was saying. I had drifted into a state that was very unfamiliar to me. My body was still planted firmly on the floorboards below me, but my head seemed to be somewhere else. I could barely hear anything, because my heart was pounding so loudly! *Goodness! Could he hear it also?* I took a deep breath and brought my head back to my body just as Julie entered the room.

"Jenny!" she cried. Julie ran to me and we held each other tightly for several minutes. She was still just as beautiful as ever. I turned my eyes back on the heavenly creature at the soda fountain. Julie noticed my obvious attraction and introduced me to him. He was J.C. Keller and an assistant manager to Uncle Frank. Having J.C. running the register freed Frank up to do more administrative duties, and J.C. was obviously a good salesman to have on the floor. I had a feeling that Frank's female customers had increased by quite a bit since this young man was hired.

After our introduction, Julie saw no reason to hang around J.C. anymore and she pulled me upstairs to her room. J.C.'s stunning blue-green eyes followed me all the way up the stairs. As I gazed backwards, I thought to myself that this would be a most memorable visit!

Julie and I had grown up very differently. While Julie was going to school and attending dances, I was keeping house and baking bread. While she wore dresses ordered from the Sears and Roebuck catalog, I sewed my own cut from my mother's dress patterns, sometimes made from the fabric of my mother's dresses. Julie's life was like a dream to me! I didn't begrudge her one bit of it. I was just happy to be able to peer into it once in a while as a dreamer peers into a fantasy for a moment of respite from reality.

Julie's bedroom was papered in pink roses and yellow daisies. A lovely porcelain doll with blonde curls and a lacy blue dress lay on top of a white chenille spread that covered her bed. The four-poster maple bed matched her dresser and vanity. That vanity was the most beautiful thing I'd ever seen. Two drawers on either side flanked a large round center mirror. Atop the drawers were little crocheted dresser scarves to protect the lovely maple wood. On each side a small cut glass lamp with a delicate lamp shade rested on the scarf along with precious little bottles of perfumes and glass powder jars. Scattered here and there, as if they were too numerous to hide, were shiny pins and hair combs with rhinestones and pearls. Whenever I visited, I just had to sit on the little tufted stool to gaze into the mirror and pretend I was a princess. I would dab a bit of perfume on my neck from one of the tiny glass jars and marvel at the dazzling jewelry.

It occurred to me at that moment how funny life was. Julie walked among these things every day and thought nothing of them. To me, they were like Wonderland! I thought about how many of us never see the real treasures that are right before our eyes. How much sweeter life would be for all of us if we did. I thought, too, that I should remember to move a little more slowly through my own life and savor every morsel, instead of flitting by it and leaving it unnoticed. I didn't have a lovely four-poster bed or beautiful things lying around my room, but I had a bed. I had four walls and a roof over my head. It was more than many people those days had. I heard stories of cities where people stood in breadlines and children begged for food on the street corners. I was so grateful that God had given me a simple life and the few things that I truly needed to be happy.

Julie flopped down onto her four-poster bed and I flopped down next to her. "I'm so glad you're here, Jenny. We are going to have so much fun!" We jumped up and down on her bed and giggled like we were 10-year-olds again. This was going to be a fun visit. The girlish joys were still there!

Julie had big plans for my visit. She was going to take me around and introduce me to all of her friends and all of the young interesting men in town. But there was only one man in town I was interested in learning more about. Once again, Julie had a treasure right under her nose and she couldn't even see it. Lucky for me that J.C. held no charm for her, or I would have never stood a chance.

In Julie's mind, J.C. was not worth bothering with. He was a stranger who wandered into town six months ago and had taken a job as a store clerk. There was no promise in that for Julie. She was looking for a little more excitement than marrying a man who worked for her father. She was looking for someone with enough ambition to carve out a life that would afford her what she was already accustomed to. She wanted to travel and go to parties. Responsibilities that tied her down were not a part of her plans.

Naturally, Julie was surrounded by young men everywhere she went. She was still as sweet and unspoiled as ever. Her sister, Viola, was a different story. Viola had never been quite as charming as Julie was and I think she was jealous of the attention that Julie commanded without any effort. In order to counteract this, Viola had taken to being somewhat aggressive in her personality. She wore tighter, flashier dresses than most of the girls did. She wore make up too. She never left the house without her face painted and her hair teased and combed up fancy. A lot of rumors floated around that town about Viola Smith. I really didn't know just how much of it was true, but from the looks of her it wasn't hard to believe. I was glad that Julie had not become what I saw in her sister.

I had never given my future much thought. I never decided what kind of man I would marry. I guess I thought that somehow marriage just happened. I didn't know how my mother met my father. My mother left me too soon to share her tales of early womanhood and romance with me. Romantic love was a complete stranger to me. I had no idea of what it was or how it felt. Still I couldn't get the thought of that beautiful young man downstairs out of my head. All of a sudden attraction was knocking on my door and I was definitely interested in getting to know it better. Once again, I wished my mother was with me to give me some guidance. I needed someone to share my confidence with. Julie was the closest thing to a sister I would ever have. She would have to be my confidant and advisor in these matters. She eagerly agreed to help me catch the eye of the mysterious lovely J.C.

Chapter 3

His name was John Christopher Keller, but everyone called him J.C. Both of us had been named one thing and called another. We already had something in common! I eagerly pointed this out to him as we conversed over the candy counter the next day. He was tall, a little over 6 feet and lean. His dark hair was already beginning to thin on top at his tender age of 23, but I thought it only accentuated his extraordinary eyes. Equally extraordinary was his crooked smile that he flashed when he asked me to the midsummer dance. I was astounded that he had asked me and certain that Julie had played some part in putting that notion into his head. Sounding quite anxious, I'm sure (I was too young and naïve to know how to be coy), I said yes right away. I floated for days on his invitation.

The night of the dance was rather warm as we walked down Main Street toward the event.

I was wearing one of Julie's dresses and a pair of pink sandals that pinched my feet. The borrowed sandals complemented the pink daisies in my borrowed dress so well that it was worth the pain. Julie talked me into bobbing my hair and I was glad. My hair naturally fell in soft waves against my face and for the first time in my life, I felt pretty. The weight of my long braids removed had given me a new energy. I held my head high and smiled as I strolled down the street in Julie's shoes.

J.C. took my hand when we crossed the street. As his fingers touched mine, the touch of his hand sent warm waves up my arm and into my body like electricity. *Was this really happening to me?* If I was dreaming, I didn't want to wake up.

The dance was held at Main Street's end on the edge of town. There were light bulbs strung on wires all around the "dance floor" made of plywood. The local ladies' group had decorated tables with flowers from their own gardens and brought homemade pies and cakes for refreshment. A fruity red punch filled a large glass punch bowl and my date and I shared a glass before stepping out onto the dance floor. It was a magical night! I danced with J.C. in those pinchy pink sandals and loved every moment of it.

Dancing really brought out the heat of the night and we decided to take a walk by the lake to cool down. We wandered off into the park. The soft coolness of the earth felt soothing to my tired and already blistered feet as I slipped off my sandals and walked down the dirt path. Across the lake we could still hear the music from the guitars and fiddle. Folks were laughing and dancing in the glow of light surrounding their party.

J.C. and I sat on a large rock next to the lake, and he put his arm around me. Again, the electricity flowed right through me! At such a tender age I'd known nothing like this before. I nestled even closer into his arm and rested my cheek on his chest. I felt safe there. We sat there staring into the night sky and enjoying the contentment of just being in each other's company. J.C. brought his left hand up to caress my cheek, then under my chin to lift my face. He looked into my eyes as he brought his face closer to mine. Before I knew it, our lips were touching, and then pressing tightly.

I will never forget our first kiss, which was my very first kiss. The warmth of his soft lips touching mine was a feeling I would conjure up in my memory time after time. His lips parted and his tongue found its way into my mouth. The more I felt of J.C., the more I wanted of him. I could feel my heart pounding wildly as his kisses awakened feelings inside of me that I had never known before.

We must have sat there on that rock in the park and kissed for half an hour. He would stop every so often and just gaze into my eyes. What was this magical power he had over me? I felt just like melted butter in his arms. The attraction between our two bodies was accelerating, and just when I thought I might explode from overwhelming desire, J.C. stopped. "I think I better take you home" he said, and kissed me very gently on my forehead as if I was a little girl. On the walk home my heart was truly a-flutter and I wondered if I might be in love with J.C.

J.C. and I were together for the rest of the time I was in Marion. His sparkling smile continued to melt me, and I was completely his.

We went to dances on warm summer nights and picture shows on an occasional rainy evening. I greeted each sunny summer morning with such glee and anticipation of my nightly date with him. I loved being in love! My loneliness seemed to have disappeared and my emptiness was filled.

Time passed quickly and summer faded. It was time for me to return home. For a while I'd forgotten that my reality was not the same as Julie's. For a brief moment, I was a young girl with nothing more on her mind than what dress she should wear for which party. One thing was for sure, I was not the same young woman who had come to town four weeks earlier. I had seen another side of life that was colorful, playful and exciting. It was tempting to stay in this new world I'd found, but responsibilities were calling me home.

J.C. promised he would come to visit me in the country soon. His promise gave me enough hope to hold onto as I made my way back, and that anticipation kept the warmth in my days as August turned cooler and days became noticeably shorter.

September came and October and still no word from J.C. The darker the days became, the darker my hopes for his visit. I still couldn't get him out of my mind, no matter how hard I tried. As I rolled out biscuits in the cool dark mornings, I imagined that I was making the biscuits for his breakfast. When I was washing the clothes, I wished they were his clothes and our children's clothes. I made every effort to make my cooking and baking the best it could be, so that someday I could please J.C. with my talents. Every evening I prayed that soon I would share my bed with this wonderful man. We would have a family of our own and live happily ever after. I would never be alone again. I waited and I wished and I prayed, but no letters came and no J.C. came knocking at my door.

Chapter 4

Julie's birthday was in October and she invited me to Marion for her party. It was by far the biggest birthday party I had ever attended and I enjoyed it very much. She loaned me a burgundy velvet gown with white lace trim on the collar and sleeves. She would never say it out loud but I knew that she loaned me her clothes so I would fit in better with her friends. I didn't mind. My feet were spending the evening in Julie's dyed-to-match burgundy satin slippers. Once again, she had succeeded in making me feel just like a princess! It was fun to be in Julie's shoes again, if only for a short time.

Having a room full of people was very exciting, but I was still very much alone, because the one person I wanted to be with,

J.C., was not in attendance. Julie told me that he had been invited, but he just hadn't shown. *Had he found another girl?* I wondered. I couldn't bear to think it. I wandered off into a corner after cake was served and stewed about where J.C. might be and all the possibilities as to why he wouldn't show up. I thought that I had meant as much to him as he did to me. He seemed so sincere about his feelings for me this past summer. Had his feelings cooled with the temperature? Had it really been a dream from which I was just now awakening?

My thoughts were going in places I didn't want to go. J.C. was a very handsome young man. Why would he bother waiting around for someone like me? I was a simple country girl, an eighty-cent bus ride away. All the while he is living in town surrounded with beautiful young women just waiting for an invitation from him. In fact, he could go out with a different girl every night if he wanted to.

I was driving myself crazy with self pity when Julie came in to check on me. She stooped down and put her arm around my shoulder. "Honey, there's someone here who wants to see you." I looked up with just the smallest tears in my eyes to see J.C. standing in the doorway.

"Hey, Jenny," he said smiling. I jumped up, ran across the room and threw my arms around his lovely neck! All was right with the world now. It could continue spinning! My love was back! It felt good to be back in his arms and to feel his kiss on my lips again. The rest of the evening flew by with delight.

As the party began to wind down, J.C. asked me to slip out the door with him. I quickly accepted his invitation to be alone. We walked along the streets of Marion hand in hand until my satin-wrapped toes were numb. The October night was cold and reminding me that even colder weather was on its way. Somehow it didn't seem nearly as dreadful as it usually did to me. Probably because the man I loved was walking through it with me.

J.C. took me to his apartment to warm up. His place was very small, but I suppose it was enough for a bachelor. He had a small area that served as a kitchen with an oven and a refrigerator. In the middle of the room sat a table and 2 chairs. Off to one side was a bed and a little dresser for his clothes. There was no couch, so J.C. and I sat on the edge of his bed. He put his arm around me and gently kissed me.

"Jenny," he whispered, I've missed you so much."

"I've missed you too," I said as we continued to kiss gently and tenderly.

The kissing grew more passionate as J.C. held my head in his hands. I could feel the warmth of his body travel all through me, as J.C. pushed his tongue between my lips. His warm, soft tongue felt amazing as it explored every inch of my mouth. I felt myself grow more excited with this kiss, and my tongue wanted desperately to be in his mouth as well. I felt our bodies slipping down onto the bed. J.C.'s body was now fully on top of mine, pressing hard. His hands were all over me—first stroking my hair and then sliding down my neck and onto my breasts.

I couldn't believe how my body was reacting to all of this touching and kissing. My breasts tingled as he held them in his hands. The tingles multiplied and continued down into my legs.

Soon, I felt his hand begin to pull my borrowed dress up over my thighs and then rest in between my legs. It was like a fire there! I felt an incredible heat between my legs and I grew very wet.

My white panties were down around my ankles before I knew it, and J.C. was pulling my legs apart. I didn't really know what was happening to me at this point. No one had ever explained to me that this was something people did. But it felt so good that I didn't want it to stop. I felt J.C.'s finger go up inside me, and I felt more heat between his fingers and my body. The next thing I knew he was inside me. Our bodies were on fire now. Our breathing was heavy and fast as J.C. continued to push himself in and out of me. It went faster and faster. It felt so good I thought my head would explode! Our bodies rocked together as one. The heat was intense and our tears of sweat intermingled as did every other part of us. I felt sounds leaving my mouth and joining with J.C.'s moans of passion. Even our very breaths were seeking each other to dance in pleasure! Then—just like that—it stopped.

J.C. rolled off of me and onto his back, exhausted. I lay there with my panties still clinging to one ankle. Julie's beautiful dress was up around my neck as a soft liquid heat began to leak out my body from between my legs. I stared up into space still a bit confused about what I had just experienced. We lay there for quite sometime just looking up at the water-stained ceiling and holding hands. Then we got up, put our clothes back on, and he walked me home.

The next day I was on a bus back home. Julie saw me off and there was no sign of J.C. My emotions were as cold and gray as the morning. The night before may have been the greatest night of my life, but today was the worst. I held back my tears, because I couldn't bear to let anyone on the bus see me crying.

Route 13 from Marion to Harrisburg is a nice, straight four-lane highway these days. Back then it was a narrow twisted two-lane road with lots of hills and valleys along the tree-lined way. In fact, it was also known in those parts that bootleggers ran through that area. Charlie Birger was the gang leader who caused quite a stir in Southern Illinois. In 1924 Charlie established a hangout called the Shady Rest right there on Route 13. Bootleggers would stop on their way to and from St. Louis on their whiskey runs. Eventually Charlie was arrested and hanged in Benton, Illinois in 1928, but his criminal activity provided the folks of Williamson County with some amazing stories. So much of a celebrity he was in those parts, there is an historical marker on the old Route 13 indicating the spot where the Shady Rest once stood.

In October of 1923, however, Route 13 was nothing more than a black winding path taking me farther and farther away from the man I loved. The sky was white with patches of gray. The orange and yellow leaves that were so beautiful just a few days before had blown off and were scattered along the road, no longer fall's delight but rather a symbol of the sadness that was in my heart. I kept my head either facing out the window or down to avoid eye contact with anyone for the entire ride to the Ozark Road, which was my stop. I had plenty of time to cry on the long walk to the house.

While walking home, I stopped at the cemetery and knelt before my mother's grave.

"Mom, I wish you were here now to tell me what to do," I said as my hands caressed her cold gray head stone. "Mom, did you ever feel this way? What do I do now? I love him and I'm so angry that he doesn't seem to feel the same. I feel so powerless! Oh, Momma! I need you!" My tears gushed out of my eyes as I wailed for her guidance. There was no answer. Only a cold wind whistled through the branches of the cedar tree and across my innocent tear-stained face.

Eventually I grew tired of hearing myself cry. I caught my breath, wiped my face with my coat sleeve and continued my walk home. It was dark by the time I reached the end of the Hunting Branch Trail. My father barely looked up as I entered the house. Katie ran for me and hugged me snugly around my waist. The warmth of the coal stove stole the hard chill from my body. Without the need to fight the cold any longer, I grew tired quickly. I went to bed without a word to anyone.

I woke up to see these two women still standing in front of me. *How long had they stood there and stared at me while I re-visited my childhood?* My daughter, Ellie, continued to explain my need to be here in order to heal the burns I had sustained. I would only be here for a short while, she said, and then I would be going home. *Good!* I thought. Hospitals can be so depressing, especially when you're old. I'd never spent much time in a hospital. I had always been very healthy and rarely ever sick. How I hated to be sick.

Time dragged by slowly while I didn't hear a word from J.C. Just a week before my birthday I came down with a terrible flu. Everyone else had seemed to escape it but me. Everything I ate had to come right back up again. I assumed that my emotions had taken their toll on my body. But after feeling so poorly for two straight weeks, my dad decided it was time to bring in the doctor

After he examined me, the doctor called my father into the room. He announced to both of us that I was going to have a baby. I lay there on the bed with my mouth open in shock. My eyes traveled from the doctor over to my father and landed on his face. My father's heartbreaking eyes grew even darker than usual at this news. He flashed an angry look at me, then at the doctor and walked out the door. I heard the front door slam as he left the house. The doctor asked me if I knew who the father was. I nodded, "Yes". Tears welled up in my eyes and began to stream down my cheeks and into my ears. The doctor turned and walked out the bedroom door and out of the house.

The next 2 weeks were miserable. I was nauseous, so I ate, then I threw up, then I was nauseous again. I struggled to get all my household chores done while I suffered through this sickness. My father would not say a word to me. He wouldn't even look at me.

It broke my heart to see my father so disappointed in me. I had always tried my best to do what was right. I worked hard to make a good home for him and my brother and sister. But now all of that was erased. I was a tragic disappointment—an unwed pregnant daughter. How could he ever forgive me?

Although he was upset, I couldn't help thinking that a baby could be an answer to my prayers. It meant that J.C. and I would get married and begin our own family just as I had dreamt of it happening for many months. There was only one problem. J.C. didn't know I was pregnant and I still hadn't heard anything from him. I wrote a letter to him and told him about my condition and then I waited.

Chapter 5

It was Christmas Eve and the sickness was starting to let up a bit. My brother and sister were giddy with the excitement of Christmas. My sister Katie was 10 and still enthralled with the magic of the holiday. Getting things ready for her kept a little of the magic alive for me also. I looked forward to the happiness in her eyes on Christmas morning when she opened the new dress I had made for her, the storybook that Charles had purchased for her, and father would definitely have some little surprise for her also.

It was 5:00 and already dark. The air was starting to become misty and soon the mist turned into a spit, then a light snow. There would be a white Christmas this year. I placed my hand on my belly and thought about next year's Christmas. There would be a baby.

Would there be a daddy? I remembered all my summer hopes of J.C., me and our children. It all seemed so long ago now. I still hadn't received a reply from my letter. I wondered if it had reached Marion safely. Perhaps it was lost and J.C. had no idea that I was pregnant. Maybe he had read the letter and left town. It was excruciating not knowing one way or the other.

My father was sitting in a chair next to the stove to stay warm. He was holding his Bible and trying to fight nodding off while he read. Charles was reading a story to Katie by the dim light of an oil lamp, and I was finishing up a pot of beans and ham for our supper. I was so distracted by my thoughts that I didn't even hear the first knock on the door. When the second knock came, I looked up startled. We all took turns looking at each other with surprised expressions. Who would be coming to the door on Christmas Eve?

I wiped my hands on my apron and walked across the room to the door. I stopped to check my hair in the little mirror on the wall by the door. I smoothed my hair, more out of nervous habit than anything. I was still keeping it short, which only infuriated my father more. There wasn't anything I could do these days to please him. My deep set eyes looked even more sunk in after having been ill for so long. My cheeks were hollow and my skin was very pale. This was not a face of a 17 year old, I thought to myself.

Turning my attention back to the door, I put my hand on the knob and turned it. I tried to think of who might venture out in this weather. It was probably a neighbor stopping by to wish us a Merry Christmas. I hoped that I wouldn't be forced to invite them to partake of our measly pot of beans for supper. It would be embarrassing to have so little to offer on such a special night. I told myself to forget my pride and open the door to whoever might be standing out there freezing in the night air. I pulled the door open only slightly until the light from inside the house shone on the person standing on the porch. The light revealed two unforgettable eyes, a nose and a crooked smile that said, "Merry Christmas, Jenny". It was J.C.

I stood there for a moment just staring at him unable to move. I couldn't decide what my next action should be. All that stood between the man who was the father of my child on the porch and my angry father inside was the door I was holding. I glanced back into the room to see three sets of eyes on me. I looked back at J.C. "Just a minute," I said to him and closed the door. I rushed to grab my wool coat from my bedroom. I didn't say a word as I swooshed past my father, Katie and Charles. I opened the door and walked out onto the porch.

I struggled to put my coat on while never taking my eyes off of J.C. He didn't say anything, just watched in silence as I buttoned my coat and reached in my pockets for my gloves. The coat had not made a bit of difference for me. I was shaking like a leaf.

When I'd finally gotten my hands covered, J.C. reached out his arms slowly and put his hands on my arms. Neither one of us could take our eyes off the other. We were like magnets when we were together, and it was very difficult to separate us. Finally he spoke. "Jenny, are you mad at me? I'm sorry I didn't come right away. I guess…" he hesitated, "I guess I just needed some time to take in that last letter from you. Do you hate me?"

Tears started to fill my eyes. "Of course I don't hate you, J.C." I said. There were so many things I wanted to say, but I thought better to wait and see what he would say next. We broke our glance and walked down the stairs onto the lawn. The snow was still lightly falling. I looked up to feel the flakes hit my face and ask God for a little guidance as I pondered my situation.

He stopped abruptly and pulled me to him. He kissed the top of my forehead and then held me close. "I love you Jenny," he said. "I can't stand being away from you."

I pulled back slightly to see his face and said, "I love you too."

Then J.C. pulled further back and lowered himself on one knee to the wet grass below us. "Jenny," he said, "will you marry me?"

I stared down at this beautiful man who was kneeling in the snow and kissing my gloved hands. I couldn't have wished for anything more magical than this moment. I could no longer feel the snow or the cold. I felt as if a fire was warming me from within. It was so strong I was sure that rays of light were shooting out all around us and lighting up the dark night. This was all I ever wanted for Christmas—a life with J.C. I smiled at my good fortune and said, "Yes".

He rose up and we kissed. We kissed and kissed again out there on that most holy night. What a beautiful sight we must have been…the two of us with child standing under a snow filled sky with nothing but our love to cling to. We stood out there and held each other and kissed until we couldn't feel our lips anymore. Then we walked up to the house where I introduced my fiancé to my father.

Chapter 6

J.C. and I married in front of the judge in Marion. Uncle Frank and Aunt Sarah stood up for us. My father, still upset over the whole thing, was absent. I didn't care that much. I was so happy to become Mrs. J.C. Keller! It was all I ever wanted. Now I would make my dreams of caring for him and our children a reality. I would have the family that I'd hoped for!

Uncle Frank gave J.C. a pay raise since he was now family and I found a job cleaning house for an elderly couple. The man's wife had taken ill and was bed-ridden. So I washed their clothes and scrubbed their floors and even cooked a meal for them now and then. I felt sorry for the man. He seemed very kind and so lonely. His wife was very distant and rarely spoke a word to me. I wondered if it had something to do with my being pregnant. The couple had no children of their own, and it may have been a reminder of the loneliness that prevailed in their relationship. Nevertheless, it was a job and good money for my family's future. Soon we would have everything we needed.

The dream life that I had always pictured faded rather quickly after our wedding. Life with J.C. was changing all the time. He stayed out later and later every night. He drank a lot. His happy-go-lucky charm that had once captivated me was slowly disappearing just as quickly as my belly was growing. I could feel him slipping away. I knew that fatherhood and the responsibilities that went along with it was not something that fit into his life. I could see it in his not-so-extraordinary glance. There was no magic when he looked at me anymore.

Hoping things would change, I ignored the sadness in his expression and continued on with my days in a normal fashion. I kept myself busy with cleaning and cooking. I pretended not to be bothered when J.C. didn't come home from work, but came in several hours later with whiskey on his breath. I'd just heat up his supper and put it on the table for him without a word.

On nights that he came home really late, I'd pretend I was already asleep. I cried quietly so he wouldn't know how much I hurt. I made believe that he wasn't slipping away, but it was difficult to convince my heart that my husband didn't love me anymore.

Something began to shift as the spring arrived. As the weather warmed, so did J.C. There was a noticeable change in his attitude by the time April rolled around. He was smiling more and he even came home at a decent hour occasionally to have supper with me. We started talking again, even laughing, and discussing plans for the baby that would be coming soon. At first I was afraid to think that I might actually have the old J.C. back, but eventually I gave in to his overwhelming charm. I felt the weight of worry beginning to lift from my shoulders. That was a great relief, because the weight in my tummy was increasing enormously.

The month of May showed up in sultry style. At J.C.'s suggestion we planned a trip to visit my family for the annual Memorial Day gathering in Ozark. Every Sunday before Memorial Day since I could remember we have gathered in the little cemetery with our families. Some would come with picnic lunches, others had entire family reunions right there on the grounds. The adults would all gather under the shade of the hickory trees to welcome each other back, to catch up on news from the year past, comment on how none of them looked any older despite the fact that the children had all grown. About 1:00 the church bell would ring to call everyone to gather inside the church for the annual meeting. We'd sing a few hymns before the meeting was called to order and we'd find out how much money we had raised to help pay the bills. It eased some of the harshness of the early summer heat to think about standing under the shade of some hickory trees out in the country. I eagerly agreed to the trip.

Things were really starting to fall together for us. Whatever roller coaster ride we had been on during the winter months seemed to have come to an end, and I was becoming optimistic again about our little family we would soon be.

J.C. purchased two bus tickets for the ride to the Ozark Road and arranged for some friends of his to pick us up in a car to drive us out the rest of the way. I was really looking forward to this trip. It was not only a chance to relax, but also an opportunity to establish some peace between us and my father before the baby came. I could feel my world was about to change tremendously.

I neatly packed my clothes in my tiny suitcase. J.C. had his own bag on that Saturday morning as we headed to the bus station. We stepped onto the bus and found two seats together midway back. I sat down next to the window and J.C. sat down next to me.

"Jenny," he said. I turned around to face him with a huge smile on my face. But I was disappointed to see that he didn't return the smile. Instead he knitted his brow and looked very serious.

"Jenny, I've got to go."

I looked at him in confusion. "What do you mean you have to go?" I asked.

"This just isn't for me. This life, fatherhood and such is just not what I want. You need to go back to your family. I need to be free. I love you, Jenny, but I can't do this anymore."

The words were still falling out of his mouth as he stood up and backed his way off of the bus leaving me sitting there stunned. The bus doors closed and we began to move. I sat there in disbelief and stared out the window at my husband making his escape from our life together. I turned to see several passengers looking at me. I pretended not to notice their pitiful stares. I refused to acknowledge that I was a big, homely, pregnant woman whose husband just left her.

With every fiber in my being I forced my tears to stay behind my eyes. I would not let those strangers take pity on me. I sat face forward and never changed my glance until the bus stopped on Route 45 at the Ozark Road. Naturally there was no car and no "friends" to give me a ride, so I began to walk down the dusty gravel in black lace up shoes that were now too small for my swollen feet. I headed towards my childhood home, my father and a very uncertain future.

Chapter 7

I had just finished my dinner tray, when my granddaughter came into my room. She looked so cheery. "How are you feeling, Grandma?" she asked. I told her I felt fine, but could she tell me why I was here? She proceeded to tell me about a fall I had in the middle of the night and that they had brought me here in a helicopter. I was in the burn unit of the hospital because I had 2nd degree burns on my chest sustained from lying unconscious on a furnace grate. I couldn't remember any of that. I knew that the large furnace grate on my floor was very hot when the furnace was on. It could melt a shoe sole if you stood on it too long. I couldn't imagine how badly I must have burned my skin if I was lying on it. I tried to look at my chest, but it was covered with bandages.

My granddaughter took out some photographs from her purse. "Would you like to see some pictures, Grandma? I just had these developed."

I agreed, and she laid them in front of me to see. "This one is from last Christmas. See, there are Debbie and Bobby."

I nodded in recognition though I was sure I'd never seen these people before. Then she put another picture down. It was of a small boy with white blond hair and blue eyes. I was sure I recognized him! I looked up at her with such enthusiasm and said, "That's Jack!"

Her face went pale, her smile dimmed, and I believe I saw tears well up in her eyes as she said, "No, Grandma. That's my son Michael, your great-grandson." She was trying very hard not to show her disappointment at my lack of memory, I know. I felt bad for her, but I just couldn't remember. I looked again at that picture of the little boy who apparently was my great-grandson. He had the same white hair and the same blue eyes. I remembered him, not as my great-grandson, but my own son, Jack. *He looked like Jack*, I thought to myself. I leaned back against my pillow with a sigh.

"It's OK, Grandma. You rest now. You're just tired." My granddaughter tried to reassure me. The thing is I wasn't upset that I couldn't remember. I was just sighing at what I did remember of Jack and his entrance into the world. A lump came to my throat as I thought of my first born.

My baby was born in late July in Ozark. I named him John Christopher after his daddy, but it wasn't long till we all called him Little Jack. I moved back in with my dad, sister and brother right after J.C. left us and just before Jack was born. It was good to be home again and have family to help out with the baby, but it was apparent that I couldn't stay forever. My father would never forgive me for what I'd done and the large valley of silence between us was more than I could take.

At first it was very difficult. It felt like J.C. had died. Sometimes it felt like he had never even existed, except the child in my arms kept reminding me that he had been real. I remembered how good it felt to have him lying next to me in bed. I missed kissing him. I missed the life I had planned out for us in my head. I thought about him when I was alone at night. I wondered if he was happy that he chose to leave. I wondered if I was dead to him like he felt to me. I wondered if I could ever really let him go. I was angry for having my happiness snagged away from me.

It took me a while of wallowing in self pity before I realized that my happiness hadn't been stolen at all, but that I'd let it walk out the door with J.C. He hadn't taken my dreams either. My ability to dream was still within me, and once I was able to figure that out, I was ready to go back and claim my happiness.

When Jack was 10 months old, I decided I had to go back to work for the couple whose house I cleaned in Marion. I needed to make some money, so Jack and I could have a house of our own someday. Unfortunately the lady of the house would not allow me to bring Jack there to live with them, so I painfully left him behind with my dad and sister to look after him. *It's just for a little while*, I told myself, *just for a little while until I can get on my feet.* I went back to Marion on my own, worked for the week and came home on the weekends.

Little Jack grew quickly in those 5 days between the weekends when I saw him. Every Friday, my heart was filled with anticipation as I hopped a bus down into the country. And every Sunday my heart felt as though it would come right out of my throat as I said goodbye to him. Unlike his daddy, Jack had a shock of white hair and fair skin. His eyes were J.C.'s blue-green though, the color of spring. He was the light of my life. I prayed that I would soon find a way for us to live together in the same house and that he would never remember the time that we were apart.

I took advantage of those weekends together. There was so much to do in the country and every reason to avoid my father, so Jack and I spent most of our time together enjoying the beauty of the area. I watched Jack climb over the monstrous rocks of limestone that emerged from sparkling pools of clear water. The land was rampant with hills, valleys, and trails. Deer, turkey, and other wildlife could always be seen just beyond the next bend. Jack and I splashed in the springs of Bell Smith and hiked down the many foot paths. Our voices joyfully rang in echoes between the cliffs, as Jack would yell, "Mom! Look at me!" and I would say, "I see you Jack! Now come down from there before you fall!"

My days were still filled with cleaning and cooking, just as they had always been since I was 11 years old, but at least now I was being paid for it. It kept my mind and body occupied during the day, so I wouldn't dwell on how much I missed Jack. The nights were empty and lonely, and I usually cried myself to sleep. Sometimes, to help, I would imagine the little house that I would get for us. I would picture us in our sunny yellow kitchen laughing and talking while I made dinner. *Soon, Jack, soon we'll have a place of our own*, I thought. I'd fall asleep with that picture in my mind.

Chapter 8

Sunday morning was when Jack and I would stroll down the country road together to church. It was one of my favorite times because it was just us. We had the road to ourselves and it seemed like all the time in the world to chat. This particular morning was in the summer, but it wasn't very hot, which was unusual for late June. I was wearing one of my favorite dresses. It was white with little daisies printed on it. It was unusual for me to wear white or anything very fancy, but today I was feeling more light-hearted than normal, and I felt like dressing up. I strolled down the road in my heavenly white dress and matching white sandals escorted by my favorite beau.

It was very still this morning. The only sound was of the gravel crunching underneath the shoes of Virginia and Jack Keller as we walked to Olive Baptist Church. Most people today couldn't imagine the quiet—the extreme quiet—of the country. Today there are so many sounds happening all the time that we don't even realize that they are there. Imagine if there were no telephones ringing, no air conditioning running, no refrigerators humming, no jets flying, no cars, nothing, just complete silence. Sometimes the silence is so strong, it is almost deafening.

As we rounded the corner near church, Jack pierced the silence I was enjoying with a loud yell, "Sam! Hey look, Mom, it's Sam!" he pointed up to the little white house on the hill to our left. There was a man with bright red hair wearing overalls and carrying a hoe working in his garden. I didn't recognize him. Jack yelled again, "Sam!" The red-headed man looked up this time from his work and upon recognizing Jack he yelled back and waved, "Hey, Jack!"

Jack grabbed my hand and dragged me up the hill. "Mom, come on. You've got to meet my friend, Sam!" I allowed my son to pull me along all the while wondering who this stranger was that appealed so much to Jack. Since I spent so much time away from Jack during the week I felt compelled to investigate the company he was keeping. As we got closer, the stranger seemed to become more familiar to me. I could see in his eyes, he was wondering, too, who I was.

"Mom," said Jack, "this is Sam. He's my friend. We hang out and talk about man things and we go fishing…" Jack was a little out of breath from running up the hill and he ran out of air mid-sentence, so Sam chimed in, "Hi, I'm Sam Reeves and I am a friend of Jack's, and you are?" He stuck out his hand in greeting.

"I'm Jack's mom, Virginia, uh Virginia Keller."

Sam Reeves? Oh my, I thought to myself. The Reeves brothers were quite a group. With 5 brothers in the family, they were their own gang. George, Billy, Norbert, and Joe were all basically the same. They were good looking men that liked to have a good time. By "good time" I mean they liked to drink, they liked women, and they liked to fight. There wasn't another batch of more hot-tempered, handsome and well-liked young men in Pope County than the Reeves brothers.

Then there was their brother Sam. Sam was a little different. He still had that fiery temper that went along with his red hair, but it took more to provoke Sam than it did the other boys. Sam was a thinker—quiet. I liked him best of the entire Reeves' boys. I remember Sam Reeves from when I was a little girl. He seemed so much older than I back then. I was 6 and he was 15. To me, he was a grown up. He was nice to me, too—nicer than his brothers were. He would always say, "Hello, Miss Virginia," when he saw me. The other boys would just as soon kick me down the street! The other thing I liked about Sam was that he never called me Jenny, like everybody else. To him, I was always Miss Virginia. As a child it made me feel older. As an adult it made me feel special.

He never seemed to mind if I tagged along behind him. I'd ask him, "Where you goin' Sam?" And he would say, "I'm goin' down to the river to fish." I'd say, "Can I go with you, Sam?" He'd say, "Someday, Miss Virginia, when you're older." "OK, Sam" I'd say and wander off home wishing I could get older really fast. By the time I was older, he was gone.

I'd heard that Sam, Billy and George had gone up north to look for factory work. I really never thought I'd see him again. Sam's brother, Norbert had been dating Julie for several months and they had recently become engaged to be married in the fall. I'd seen Norbert with Julie a few times, but I'd never thought to inquire about Sam. It had been 10 years since the last time I saw him and I was 10. I'd probably changed a little since he'd seen me last. I guessed that was why he was looking at me now so intently.

"Sam Reeves," I said. "It's been a long time, hasn't it?"

"Virginia Keller?" He rolled his eyes back into his head as if he were trying desperately to remember my name and how he could know me while he wiped the sweat from his freckled face with his handkerchief. He was studying me up and down. I was glad that I had on my prettiest dress and shoes. I felt like a gleaming white angel standing next to this dirty farm boy. There was something so satisfying to my ego to look this nice to a man whose last encounter with me was at a fishing hole as an awkward pre-teen. I was savoring every moment while he looked me over and tried to guess who I was.

I couldn't stand the anticipation any longer, so I said, "Where you goin' Sam?" in my little girl voice.

Immediately Sam said, "Miss Virginia!"

I smiled in sweet satisfaction.

"Miss Virginia, the last time I saw you..." He stopped. I think he caught himself before he said something that he thought would be unflattering. He thought again and started over, "You look wonderful."

I thanked him for the compliment. I told him that I had heard he moved up north and asked what made him return. He told me about moving up to Galena and working in a factory with his brothers. Factory work was not too appealing, even though the pay was good, and Sam had decided he needed to come back here and work the land. There was something about this beautiful country that gets into the blood of its natives. Apparently it had called Sam back. He moved into this little house on the hill just across the road and down a ways from the cemetery about six months ago. He couldn't afford to buy it, so he'd worked out an arrangement with the owner to work the land and fix up the house in return for rent. It was a nice piece of ground for farming, and with a little work, the house could be just as lovely as when it was first built. It was not large by any stretch of the imagination—just kitchen, sitting room and 2 bedrooms upstairs. But there was still something very charming about the house with its wraparound porch and impressive view of the land that I had always found appealing.

The sound of the church bell brought us back into the present world and we exchanged goodbyes and promised to get together soon to catch up. Jack and I walked into church a minute late and sneaked into a back pew. It was hard to focus on prayer that morning. I couldn't keep the smile from my face as I thought about this chance encounter with Sam. I was so pleased with myself for looking particularly attractive and handling myself with grace while conversing. But it was much more than self-satisfaction that kept that smile on my face the rest of the day. I was afraid to even admit to myself that I felt a certain attraction to this man from my past. It was as if someone had lifted a dusty old cover to reveal something polished and pretty underneath! I turned my eyes heavenward and thanked the Lord for a glorious morning!

Chapter 9

Being in the hospital for so many days had made it difficult to keep track of what day it was. I could count them only by the visits I received from my daughter or my granddaughter. They had all been in today—my daughter and her husband, my 2 granddaughters and a son-in-law. It was good to have some company and to talk and laugh. It was a tremendous contrast to the quiet of the rest of my day.

It was a weeknight, and they'd all gone home for the evening. I turned on the television, but there was nothing to watch. I couldn't stand to see the silly situation comedies that people watched these days, and the news was too depressing. I switched the T.V. off and turned off the light in my room.

It was raining and the parking lot lights were projecting rain drops onto my wall in the darkness. I liked the sound of the rain hitting the window. It was so calming to focus on the tiny sound of each water droplet as it splashed on the glass.

I imagined how cold the rain was tonight, since it was January. It must have felt like ice as it fell on my visitors making their way to their cars. I was glad to be warm and dry and safe in my bed tonight.

I watched as the reflection of the droplets ran down the window and created a moving work of abstract art for me on my hospital room wall. The wet streams running down the window danced between the light of the parking lot and the darkness of night. The tiny pattering of the raindrops was so comforting, and I slipped into a hypnotic state as I stared at the wall.

The sound of the rain grew harder as the storm picked up its intensity. I drifted further into my dream state, and pictures of an unforgettable rainstorm flooded my sight.

I had made some friends while living in Marion—Delores and Judy. Delores worked at the dress shop and Judy worked at the bank. They were longtime friends and had known each other since they were babies. I met them both at the same time one evening when I decided to treat myself to dinner at the local diner. I had just finished paying and I was on my way out the door. As I passed by their table, Delores commented on how pretty my dress was and asked me where I got it. Since she worked at the only dress shop in town, she was very curious. When I told her that I had made it myself, she was intrigued. They invited me to sit down with them and we talked for hours. From that moment on we were friends. It made such a difference in my life. Suddenly I had someone to see a picture show with or eat a meal with or just someone to talk to. Those girls will never know just how much power their presence held in my life.

Not only was their friendship a treasure to me, but it also proved fruitful in other ways. Delores was in need of a seamstress to perform alterations at the shop. So she passed on extra work to me. Judy helped me set up a little savings account at the Marion Bank and I learned how to save my money a little faster. I could feel myself really growing and taking charge of my future. I was making good decisions and I could see a better place on the other side of this dark tunnel I had been living in for quite a while now. I was happier than I'd been in a long time.

One unseasonably warm August afternoon, Judy and Delores asked me to come to their Wednesday night church services with them. I was reluctant at first, but then I thought that it might be a good opportunity to meet more friends and become more active in the community. So I agreed to meet them at a quarter to 7 that evening outside the doors of their church.

As I stepped out of the door that evening I could feel the heaviness in the air. No doubt a storm was brewing somewhere, I thought. I was always a little afraid of storms and so I said a prayer real quick just then that the storm would blow over while we were inside church and be done before we were let out. I made my way up Spring Street. The wind was beginning to gust—first a short gust, then quiet, then a longer gust of hot air. With one hand on my hat and one holding the hem of my dress, I walked down to the corner, turned left, then two blocks down to the church. There were Delores and Judy holding onto their own hats and skirts to keep the wind from revealing too much information to the general public. The sky was white and the wind was beginning to take on a steady flow now. We joined the others that were filing in quickly while giving one last gaze to the sky.

Inside, the church was very charming. It was not a large building. It probably held 100 people at the very most. I was surprised at how many people attended this weeknight service. The upright piano in the corner was being played beautifully by an older woman. Her dress was store-bought with a sweet little cherry print. On top of her white hair that was pulled back into a bun, she wore a tiny little white hat with a touch of white netting and a stem of plastic red cherries stuck to it. Her bright red lipstick smile told me that leading this evening's singing was a highlight for her. I imagined that she must be a widow and that this one night a week was what she looked forward to most in her life.

It was almost 7, so the three of us slipped into a pew about halfway up the aisle. The music played on, "What a friend we have in Jesus…" We opened our hymnals and began to sing along with the crowd. It did feel good to be there, I thought. I was glad that I decided to come out. I thought about how much I had to be thankful for. I had a beautiful son and I was making some money that would soon bring us back together. I had made some new friends that I just adored. Life was looking up for me without a doubt. The more I thought about the blessings in my life, the more I sang out. It was exhilarating to be in a room full of joyful people. It was contagious!

The song ended and all was quiet in the little church. Just then a huge clap of thunder crashed and shook the entire building. This of course jostled the congregation a bit and there was the usual low murmuring of conversation among them. I looked around at the faces as they one by one looked up at the ceiling of the church as if they expected to see a storm cloud forming above their heads instead of just a ceiling of a church. I thought it was a little funny and I let out just a tiny giggle to myself at the sight of it. The front doors blew open just then and we all turned around to see two latecomers drenched in rain water and out of breath, probably from running to make it inside before the storm hit. I could see through the door opening the rain was swirling outside. I was glad I was inside and silently thanked the Lord for delivering me here before it started.

At that point, I think the prayerful atmosphere that had been established by the lovely singing had been lost. This band of faithful servants had once again become a herd of lost sheep in tonight's storm. Just then the pastor walked out in front of the altar and brought our attention to the front of the room again. "Brothers and sisters," he began, "we have a special treat for you tonight. As much as I enjoy leading you in our normal scripture study on these Wednesday evenings, I willingly bow out to offer you a refreshing alternative. Tonight we have the pleasure to have with us one of our newest ministers of the church.

Recently ordained, he has come up from Paducah to lead us all in tonight's service. So let's make our visitor feel welcome as we greet him."

The pastor motioned as if to call the visitor out from behind the wall. Again, there was that soft muffled murmur of conversation from the congregation as they speculated why the pastor wasn't performing tonight's service and curiosity as to who this new pastor was. It really made no difference to me. I didn't know the old pastor, so a new pastor would be just fine as far as I was concerned.

The mysterious visitor came out from behind the wall. People craned their necks to see his face, and as those in front of me did, they blocked my view. "Good evening, brothers and sisters. It is a pleasure to be here with you tonight." I still couldn't see, but that voice sounded strangely familiar to me. I began to crane my neck in an attempt to see from behind a very tall man in front of me. "I see the stormy weather couldn't keep you away from your Lord and Savior tonight. Rest assured, God sees you, brother, and God is watching you, sister."

That voice! The sound of it sent a shock to my heart. I knew that voice, but I had to see to be sure. My heart was beginning to pound and my whole body was pulsating as the thought of who that could be standing in the front of this church could be. *But it couldn't be!* I struggled to see over the large man sitting in front of me, but I failed. I tried peering from side to side in between the heads, but it was still no good. Finally I couldn't take the suspense any longer. I forgot my manners and I stood straight up from my seat.

There he stood! My eyes still did not believe it. At this point all eyes—including his—were on me. You could have heard a pin drop in the quiet if it hadn't been for the rushing wind and driving rain that moved about so fiercely outside. But that monster outside was no match for the one raging inside of me at that moment. The look on his face told me that he could see the storm behind my eyes as well.

No one in the crowd had any idea why I was reacting to this new preacher. How could they? Oh, but I couldn't help myself at this point. The man standing at the altar could see very clearly the rage inside me. This man could see my very soul if he wanted to. He once held my heart in his hands. This preacher standing before me was none other than J.C. Keller, the man who broke my heart seven years ago by walking out on me and his unborn child!

As usual, where J.C. was concerned, it took me a few moments to compose myself. I courteously excused myself out of the pew past my friends and several others and walked down the aisle to the back of church. The congregation continued to stare at me, but I didn't care. I was through with appearances and worrying about what others might think. I pulled open the wooden doors. My heart continued to pound and my mind raced. The wind and rain rushed in and nearly knocked me down at first, but I recovered and walked out the door into the night. The storm raging outside no longer frightened me near as much as the quiet calm of what I was leaving behind.

The mixture of the wind, rain, lightning and my emotional state left me confused and I stood there on the sidewalk like a frightened stray dog as I waited for cooler senses to take over. I turned to my left and started running down the sidewalk toward home. As I ran, I began to cry.

I'm sure I must have looked like a lunatic had anyone actually been outside to see me soaked to the skin, running and sobbing.

I turned the corner to Spring Street and continued right. The rain was blowing right in my face now and I could barely see. The water had overcome the gutters and was now standing high on the sidewalks. As I ran I could feel the water rush into my black pumps as my heels rose out of them. Then as my heels sunk back down, the water squished its way back out. *Squish! Clunk! Squish! Clunk!* I went traipsing up the block.

My mind raced with terrible thoughts. *How dare this man come back into my life this way! A preacher—J. C.?* I still couldn't believe it all. Years of pent up anger were shooting out of me every which way it could. I was so mad at him! I couldn't believe that I had wasted any of my time worrying about him, wondering where he was, what he was doing, if he still thought about me, if he still loved me. None of that mattered at that point. I knew at that moment that I didn't love him anymore. The answer to all my questions was staring me right in the face from a church altar.

I don't know if it was my anger or my body that gave out first. It was a close race. I could hardly breathe any more. I think the rain had added ten pounds to my clothes which made it even harder to run. I was moving slower and slower. It was taking too much energy to hold up under the weight of the storm and there was little left to support my emotion, and so just like that I let it go.

I decided to give up, take it as a sign that J.C. and I were finally finished. It was time to really move on with my life and stop carrying around the hurt and the anger. Just like that as I made this decision, I felt a new energy within me.

Even the rain was touching me now in a different way than before. Instead of pelting me with pain and fueling my fire, it was now washing me clean, removing the old and the dead. The more I walked, the lighter I felt. I let it envelope me like a cleansing shower. I continued on just walking with a slight smile on my lips and I closed my eyes, enjoying the comfort of finding some peace. I was almost home now, if I could just make it one more block.

Then, out of nowhere I hit something. *Smack!* I ran right into a man on the sidewalk! *That's what I get for walking with my eyes closed!* I thought. The act of being stopped so abruptly combined with my emotional state must have been all my body could take, because the next thing I knew I was limp in this stranger's arms. I apologized as I tried to gather enough strength to pull myself away from his helpful grasp. I wiped the droplets from my eyes to look up into his face so I could thank him for his help. As I did, a flash of lightning revealed to me the stranger's identity. The unmistakable red hair and kind face belonged to none other than Sam Reeves.

The rain continued to swirl about us as Sam and I stood staring at each other at the corner of Spring Street and 5th. A loud crash of thunder sent us both looking for an awning to duck under. "Sam, what are you doing here?" I asked.

"I came here looking for you, Virginia." He replied almost yelling over the sound of the pounding raindrops. "After I met you that day out by the road with Jack, I got to thinking about you." He was intense as he went on. His eyes never left mine. It was as if he had to hold me there with his eyes until his entire message was received—like life as we knew it depended on his every word. His hands were wrapped around my arms like he was afraid to let go. I kept my eyes directly on his. Sam went on, "Virginia, I went to see your dad about a week ago. He told me all about Little Jack and how his father had left you. I couldn't stop thinking about it all. Your dad told me where you lived, but when I knocked on the door, they said you had gone out, so I just started wandering around, hoping I would eventually run into you."

He stopped speaking for a moment. He must have realized how crazed he seemed to me and decided to calm himself a bit before he went on. "How are you? Are you OK?" he asked as he scanned my face for what I'm not sure. My arms were still held tight in his grasp.

"I'm fine Sam," I replied, "but I still don't understand why you are here now. Why did you have to come looking for me?" While I was thrilled to see him, I was still very confused as to his motivation. I pulled away a little from him as a thought entered my mind. Was Sam feeling the urge to be a white knight? As a little girl I had wanted nothing more, but as a woman I had come to realize that the only person who could come to my rescue was me. He'd heard my story and what? Felt sorry for me? I decided to just put it bluntly. "You didn't come here to rescue me or anything, did you Sam? I don't need rescuing." I thought how odd that probably sounded to him coming from a woman who had just run 6 blocks in a thunderstorm, sobbing, and drenched to the bone.

Sam didn't even blink. He just kept staring into my eyes. *Hazel brown*, the thought jumped into my head as I stood staring into Sam's eyes. I hadn't noticed until just then that his eyes were hazel brown. I was thinking how nice they looked with his red hair and his sun-scorched freckled face. I became so engrossed in my own thoughts, that when he finally answered me, I'd forgotten the question.

Sam shook his head at me and said, "No, I'm not here to rescue you. I came here because I haven't been able to stop thinking about you since that Sunday that we met. I came here because I was devastated when I found out you were Jack's mom, which meant you must be married. But when your dad told me you weren't married, I was thrilled!"

He paused to catch his breath, and then went on, "I'm sorry. I know I shouldn't be happy at your unhappiness. I don't mean it like that at all. What I mean is," he took another breath, "I couldn't stop thinking about you. I couldn't fight the feelings I was having. I had to come find you, but not to rescue *you*. I'm the one who needs rescuing. I've been going out of my mind since that day I saw you. Something's eating away at my insides! It's like I'm crazy. No, you are not the one who needs rescuing. I am, Virginia Keller," he said as he put a hand on each side of my face and looked deep into my eyes and said quietly, "Will you rescue me?"

"Sam" was all I could say. I was overcome by what he had just said. I was running the gamut of emotions for the second time this evening. I felt confused, scared, exhilarated. I didn't know whether to cry, laugh or just jump at him and kiss him.

Very slowly Sam pulled my face closer to his. He ran his hands across my wet hair, caressing me like I was a lost child he'd just found. Still a little puzzled by what had just taken place; I smiled a little smile at him. I knew what Sam was talking about. I knew because I hadn't stopped thinking about him either since I saw him that day. I smiled at how I could see God's plan in my life on this stormy August evening—more than I may have ever seen it before. I lifted my face up higher and pressed my lips to Sam's in a tiny tender kiss. Sam smiled back.

We decided to get in out of the rain and found our way to the diner. We sat down and had a piece of pie and about twelve cups of coffee as we talked about old times growing up in the country and catching up on the time that had passed while we were apart. The rain continued to pour down outside, but it was warm and cozy from my seat.

Sam and I were hardly ever apart from each other after that evening. For the next few months he courted me on my weekend visits back to the country. We were married in November at Olive Church. I thank God every day for the gift He gave me when He brought Sam Reeves into my life.

Chapter 10

A woman entered my hospital room claiming to be my daughter. I really wasn't sure. Things were getting pretty muddled for me. I drifted in and out just to wake and see the same shades of white surrounding me. People came, took my temperature, checked my bandages, gave me pills, brought me food, asked about my bowels and left. I kept asking them to tell me why I was in here, but they just ignored me and went about their business.

I allowed this woman to come in and talk to me mostly because I was lonely and could use the company. She carried a photo album with her, which she presented to me. "Mom, I thought you might want to look through these photos. It will give you something to do." *Why did I need something to do in here? I needed to get out of here so I could go do the real things I needed to do.* I was sure my laundry was stacking up. The ladies at the church would be wondering when I would be back to help with quilting. I had to check on my next door neighbor. She was all alone and she relied on me to help her get her dinner prepared and her laundry cleaned and folded. I had places to be and I didn't need anything more to do.

I guess this woman could see by my wrinkled brow that I was in no mood to look at her picture album, so she set it aside. She sat down with a sigh and asked me how I was feeling. I turned my gaze away from her. *How was I feeling? How could she even ask?* For some strange reason I was in this boring hospital room being kept against my will. No one could tell me why I was here. I decided they must all be in on it together, so I wasn't going to talk to any of them. I couldn't believe anything they would have told me anyway. I just wanted to be left alone. I closed my eyes and fell asleep, I suppose, because when I opened them again, the woman was gone.

A nurse came soon after I woke up. She checked the bandages on my chest and asked if there was anything she could bring me. I rolled my head across my pillow and my eyes landed on the photo album still lying on the table. She saw my glance and walked over to the table, picked up the album and laid it on my lap. I thanked her and she left.

The album was less than ordinary, beige and covered in plastic. I opened the front cover. There was a picture of Sam and me. It brought a smile to my face immediately. Sam looked so handsome, and I looked so young! That photo must have been taken at Julie's wedding, because we didn't know anyone with a camera when we were married, so there were no photos. It might as well have been our wedding photo. We were married 7 days after Julie and Norbert. I remembered that pink dress I was wearing when the picture was made. I'd made it special for the wedding. I'd spent hours on those tiny little pleats on the bodice. It was a delicately beautiful dress, very feminine. The shoes should have been matching pink satin, but I couldn't afford new shoes, so instead I wore my black pumps.

What a time we had that night! Sam and I were so in love. Julie and Norbert was such a happy couple on their wedding day. I admired how they could laugh and tease each other all the time. Norbert was a wild man and sometimes he would drive Julie half crazy with his drinking and carrying on. Then Norb would come up and put his arms around Julie's waist and say, "Is you is or is you ain't my baby?" and Julie would have to smile and all would be forgiven for another day.

After our wedding, Jack and I moved into Sam's little white house. It was good to finally give Jack a real family. I loved my father and he was good to Jack, but it was time for my son to have a real dad and allow my dad to be a grandpa. Jack had lived so long with my father by this time, that most folks in the country thought he was my dad's son rather than mine. They often referred to him as Jack Sommers rather than his real name, Jack Keller. I offered to let Sam adopt him and change his name to Reeves, but Sam declined. He said that a man's name was the one thing that he could hold onto in this life and he could not take that away from Jack.

The first thing I did was paint the kitchen yellow. When I was working in Marion, and away from Jack, I spent so many nights fantasizing about the house I would have someday and cooking meals for Jack in my own sunny yellow kitchen. Meeting Sam and getting married had made so many of my dreams a reality. Now I spent most of my waking hours in that kitchen making meals for the two men in my life. And my nights were not wasted on fantasy, but spent in the arms of the man I loved.

It wasn't long before Sam and I were expecting our first born. We named him Curtis after my brother who had passed on as an infant. Curtis was the spitting image of Sam. His bright red hair and his strong willed disposition gave no margin of error that he was a Reeves boy. It was good for Jack to finally have a brother. Although the age difference was great, he was so good with Curtis. Jack was just as kind and patient as Curtis was stubborn and mischievous. They were a perfect complement to each other. It was a treasure to see those two running around the countryside together.

Three years after Curtis was born, we were blessed with Eleanor. She was named after my favorite aunt, Eleanor, but soon we were just calling her Ellie. She was a perfect blend of Sam and me. Her bright red curls clearly defined her as Sam's, but she had more of her mother's temperament. It was fun having a girl for a change. I enjoyed making little dresses and baby dolls for her. Ellie adored Jack. She'd follow him around the way I used to follow Sam when I was a young girl. It drove Curtis crazy mad to see his little sister tag along. He'd call her names and push her around, just like his uncles used to do with me. Jack would always come to her rescue and tell Curtis to mind his own business. Sam and I would have a good laugh watching them and remembering earlier times.

With more mouths to feed, life became a little more challenging. Sam kept up with our growing demands by taking a job at the cemetery. He mowed the grass, weeded and performed general caretaking work for a few extra dollars. The boys helped him out in the summer when school was out. He also took a job with the Civilian Conservation Corps (CCC) overseeing the planting of several hundred pine trees as part of a project to stop the natural erosion that had been occurring in our area. Sam was a natural leader with a strong sense of organization and a firm command to his voice. He did a wonderful job setting those magnificent lodge pole pines.

With the establishment of the Shawnee National Forest, the CCC was expanded and when Jack was old enough, he also joined them to work on various projects. The results of these projects can still be seen today and are enjoyed by many tourists. The fruits of Sam's and Jack's labor, along with so many others, will always be with us.

Chapter 11

My favorite season had always been the spring. The spring offered so much hope. There is nothing like the smell of the first hints of it when the earth warms just enough to release its scent. How exhilarating it is to feel the ground beneath your feet begin to wake up from its winter sleep! Somehow that awakening transfers into my body and seeps into my soul to make me feel as if I am awakening also. That feeling inspires the hope of new life and new opportunities that makes my heart dance.

Many people love the fall with its bounty of color, the crisp cool relief from summer's oppressive heat. Not me. I've never liked fall. I knew all that color and clear blue sky was just a cover for what lay ahead—winter, so I never allowed myself to enjoy it. Fall was just a sobering moment for me to realize that the frivolity of summer is passing and I must return to reality.

This particular fall day of 1941 was a moment of reality I was extremely reluctant to face. Two months after his 18th birthday, Jack received notice to report to the army camp in Fort Bragg, North Carolina. So on this crisp, clear October day, we drove Jack to the train station in Carbondale. Sam and I never owned a car, so a neighbor loaned his to us for the day. The whole family piled into this automobile— Sam, me, Jack, Curtis, and Ellie. It was a long drive from the country and I was thankful for the time to drag. I would have frozen time if I could at that moment. There I sat in the front seat between Sam and Jack. The car had no top, so the October air was brisk on our faces. I wondered if Jack could sense the dread I had of him leaving. *Did this young man sitting next to me know how much I loved him?*

I looked over at his face—his beautiful face. He truly had become a young man overnight. *Where had the time gone?* I wondered how I missed my little boy disappearing before my eyes and being replaced with a man. He was so handsome. Jack had always been a cute little boy, but now he was a striking young man. He'd gotten the best of me and his father. Jack had inherited my strong cheekbones, square chin, and his eyes were deeply set below his brow just like mine. On me, I always thought those features made me look harsh, but on Jack, it looked strong! Jack didn't have my eyes though. That Caribbean blue was definitely J.C.'s.

Jack looked over at me staring at him. His eyes seemed to say that he knew exactly what I was thinking. He smiled a little grin and I smiled back wrinkling my nose and scrunching up my eyes like I always did to hold back the anguish I was feeling.

We arrived at the train station just in time for all the children to say goodbye to their brother. Ellie wrapped her little arms around Jack's waist. "I'll miss you, Jack!" she said in her tiny voice. Of course she had no idea where he was going or for how long. Jack reached down and scooped her up in his arms. Their noses just touching, he said, "I'll miss you too, baby girl. Be good for Mama." Jack kissed his little sister on the cheek and set her down. Curtis said goodbye, then Sam, and then it was my turn.

For the first 6 years of Jack's life, it had been just him and me. And even after Sam and I were together and the other children were born, there seemed to be a special bond that existed between Jack and me. In some ways we were like brother and sister, because we'd done a lot of growing up together. Communication passed between us without uttering a word. He was a sensitive, caring boy. He was good at reading me, so I learned to guard my feelings around him. It was important to me that he, and all my children, made his own decisions based on his own knowledge. I didn't want him to see how I was affected. Today I had already decided that Jack would not see me cry. He would not sense one bit of sorrow that he was leaving. He hugged me goodbye and looked into my eyes. I gave him my best *I'm so proud of you* look. He hugged me again and boarded the train. I turned away and walked swiftly to the car. I never looked back. I couldn't. It would have been over if I had and my intention to be strong would have failed. I just kept telling myself to put one foot in front of the other and soon I was at the car.

The ride home was excruciating. The kids were noisily chattering, but I didn't hear a word. I sat there frozen in the front seat, the cold night air on my face helping me to maintain my rigidity. I dared not speak a word or move my eyes from their forward glance for fear that I would break down. I knew if I looked at Sam I'd fall apart and I needed to stay together for the sake of the kids. I refused to let them see me cry. Sam knew what I was feeling also and he kept his eyes locked on the road.

By the time we made it home, it was time for dinner, baths, and off to bed. With the children all tucked in, I walked out the back door and into the cold dark night. There must have been a million stars twinkling in that clear sky, but I didn't see them. Someone once said that having a child means knowing what it's like to have your heart walking around outside your body. That's how I felt out there on that moonlit night. My heart was hundreds of miles away from me and I felt such loss. The large lump in my throat which had kept me from eating any dinner was still lodged there. I began to wonder if it would just stay there until Jack returned.

Just then I felt the warmth of Sam's hand on my shoulder. I turned to face him. The light from the kitchen door splashed onto Sam's face and revealed tears welled up in his eyes. Seeing this emotion in him caused me to gasp, and then I pulled Sam tightly to me. His tears gave me permission to shed my own, and I began to feel some release of the self-made prison I'd been in all afternoon. We stood there, Sam and me, out there in the cold October darkness for what seemed like half the night. His arms wrapped around my waist. My arms held him tightly around his neck and my head rested on his shoulder. We stood there in each other's arms in the moonlight and sobbed like babies.

Chapter 12

That first winter without Jack was hard. I still had two children at home that gave me great joy, but there was a void left unfilled by Jack's absence. The sound of President Roosevelt's voice on the radio on the evening of December 7th filled my heart with an unmistakable dread.

Jack was in Ft. Bragg only 2 months before he was shipped overseas. Now my only contact with him was "V" mail. I received many letters from Jack that looked like Swiss cheese. Those letters with the holes looked a lot like my heart. The more holes in it, the more I worried that he was in danger. There was usually not much to them other than he loved us and missed us. He would be home as soon as this war was over.

Spring came and then summer. It was good to feel the long hot summer days again. Sam, the kids and I worked hard in that heat. There was always something to be done. We grew almost everything we ate: tomatoes, beans, carrots, potatoes, squash, cucumbers, corn, peaches, strawberries, apples and grapes. Sam usually kept a couple of hogs and butchered them in the fall. We also had some chickens for eggs and, of course, fried chicken on special days. With a growing family, we had to make things stretch as far as they could go. If we couldn't grow it or make it, we usually went without.

Julie and her husband, Norbert, had opened a tiny store not too far from us, so we were able to buy things like milk and flour without having to go all the way into town. They also built a 2 story house nearby. Besides the shopping convenience, it was nice to have Julie so close to me. They had done very well for themselves, with a little help from Uncle Frank. Their store wasn't as big as Uncle Frank's store in Marion, but it was the best this part of the country had ever seen. They sold the regular staples, like flour, milk, eggs, and canned goods. They also had a little lunch counter where Julie cooked burgers. In the corner stood a pop machine that dispensed bottles of Pepsi, Orange Crush, and root beer for a nickel. They also had 2 gas pumps out front. It was a busy little place offering so much out in the middle of nowhere.

Since we rarely had the money to spend on pop and restaurant food, our kids thought they'd died and gone to heaven when they got to visit Aunt Julie's. I liked going too. It was nice to have a place to go that was so unlike your own. Just like when we were younger, I was still peering into Julie's life. This was a place where money didn't matter, and there was an endless supply of everything. If you wanted a pop, they'd give you a nickel to pull one out of the machine. If you were hungry, you could choose from countless prepared and boxed foods on the shelves. When their kids' clothes were torn or stained, they were thrown out back and burned, and Julie would order new ones from the catalog. I was glad that Julie was happy, that Norb could give her and their 4 children so much. They always seemed so carefree.

Visiting them was definitely a treat, but it was always good to go home. As with any sweet indulgence, too much of it can spoil your appetite for the things that are truly good for you. I was thankful for all I had and didn't have. God hadn't given me riches, but He had blessed me with other gifts. I was a good cook and had become well known across the county for some of my dishes. I could make a dress for Ellie that was identical to the ones she picked out of the catalog, and I could take a torn shirt from Julie's backyard, mend it and wash it till it was as good as new for Curtis to wear proudly. I wonder if Julie ever noticed. There was a satisfaction in it that few people ever experience, I reckon. I knew it and my kids knew it.

I was startled awake—as usual—by a nurse who told me I needed to wake up and eat some lunch. Apparently a tray had been dropped off while I was dozing.

I raised my bed to bring myself up to a sitting position and the nurse pulled my tray over my lap so I could eat. Hospital food. What other adjectives were needed? The phrase speaks for itself, doesn't it?

I stared down at my tray of some kind of meat covered with some kind of sauce. Next to it was probably mashed potatoes, corn and sliced peaches. It must be yellow day, I thought to myself. Couldn't they find any other color to cook today? Nothing was very appetizing and I really didn't feel very hungry, so I decided just to eat a bit of peaches.

The cool sweetness of the peach felt good on my tongue. I chewed into the soft flesh of my first slice and let the flavor of it slowly descend my throat. Canned peaches just were no match for fresh ones. I placed another slice on my tongue and again tried to savor what little flavor there was. I closed my eyes and pictured the bright sunshine that was the color of the peach. The softness and the sweetness in my mouth conjured up a memory that I'd almost completely forgotten. I laughed to myself as I began to recall the most romantic afternoon, and the amazing role that a peach played in all of it.

I woke on the morning of July 20—Jack's birthday—feeling blue. My baby was turning 19 somewhere in the world, but not with me. I could get myself so down thinking about him. On a day like this one, I could manage to talk myself into staying in bed all day. Sam knew this about me and had counted on me needing something to cheer me up.

He surprised me by sending the children off to Aunt Eleanor's and taking me on a picnic. It was one of those rare days in July when the humidity was low and the sky was clear. Sam and I took a basket and blanket down to a place called Teal Pond where as a young girl I once followed him to watch him fish.

My blessings were many in this life, but none as great as my husband. Sam was everything I needed in a partner. He was kind and thoughtful, sensitive, and strong. He knew this day would be hard for me. He'd seen it coming and was ready to battle it head on with this surprise. It was this kind of thoughtfulness and caring that kept our relationship young and strong.

We sat on our blanket enjoying sandwiches that Sam had so carefully and quietly made while I was getting dressed, so to add to the surprise. The soft white bread melted in my mouth, and I treasured every bite. It was a rare treat to have store-bought bread and a bit canned meat. It might as well have been caviar! We washed the sandwiches down with some lemonade and lay down to soak up the sun on our faces.

If the picnic hadn't been enough of a surprise, his next actions left me completely amazed. Sam reached into the picnic basket and pulled out a peach. He took a bite and then handed it to me. I put my mouth next to the open wound Sam had just made in its flesh. My tongue savored the soft fuzziness of the peel for a moment just before my teeth sunk in and pulled the smooth, slightly stringy fruit into my mouth. The sweet juice squirted out onto my face and ran down my chin and my neck. Before I could move the peach away from my mouth, Sam bent down to my neck and began to lick the juice off my skin. His mouth made its way from my neck up my chin to my lips where he kissed me. The sweet stickiness now on both our mouths, we continued to share it.

Sam's hand ran over my cheek and down to my chest where he began to unbutton my blouse. He spread my blouse open and removed my bra. Then he took our half-eaten peach and dragged its sweetness across my chest, lingering and softly circling each breast. He brought his mouth down to suck the soft sticky fluid off my skin. His out of character behavior was driving me wild with passion!

We undressed and both walked naked into the water until we were waist-high. Sam held onto my hands as I leaned back as far as I could. He began to twirl me around in a circle. I looked up at the clear summer sky and breathed in the sweet country air. I felt more relaxed than I'd felt in years. The feeling of that cool water flowing over my body was intoxicating.

I imagined what Sam and I must look like at that moment to anyone who might take an unfortunate turn and stumble onto us. We would surely look like two pagan lovers flipping about naked in the pool! I didn't care if anyone saw us. After laughing and splashing about like children, we climbed out of the water and made love on our blanket before packing up and going home.

I felt good and alive—something I hadn't felt in many months. We walked home holding hands like young lovers. It was a beautiful end to an amazing, unforgettable day.

Nine months later, we were blessed with our third son, James.

Chapter 13

The bright sunlight coming through my window woke me up early. The unfamiliarity of sunlight in January must have startled me. I decided to revisit the photo album while I waited for my breakfast.

I turned another page of the album and found a picture of our youngest son, James when he was 16. He had dark hair like mine and his father's freckles. Unfortunately he had terrible eyesight and had to wear some horribly thick glasses by the time this picture was taken. James was a good boy, but oh did he work my nerves over the years! I thought about the many times his mischievous behavior had embarrassed me.

He was probably 4 or 5 years old when were all at church. We had arrived late and so we stood in the back. James decided to crawl under every pew until he made it up to the front at the preacher's feet. Of course, I had no idea that he'd gotten so far away from me and I was shocked when I saw him pop out from underneath the front pew.

James looked up and said, "Hey Preacher!" Everyone in the congregation laughed except for me of course. And there was no way for me to get to him, which was probably a good thing. Then the preacher asked him, "James, is that a new shirt you're wearing?" James replied, "No, Preacher, Mom just made this out of an old skirt!"

The roar of laughter from the pews was deafening and my face must have turned thirty shades of red that morning. James was lucky he was out of my reach at that moment or I'd have probably been put in jail. Sam kept us apart for the rest of the day.

The next page held pictures of Jack as a boy and as a young man. One picture was of Jack and Sam. Jack's arm was around Sam. I always liked the fact that they were friends before I had even met Sam that day. He treated Jack as if he was his own and the two were such good friends. Jack needed Sam and Sam needed him. It was a perfect fit.

A 5x7 black and white of Jack in his army uniform stared back at me on the facing page. From most people's vantage point Jack looked handsome and sophisticated. From where I stood, all I could see was my baby. As handsome as Jack was in that uniform it still brought back all those memories of worrying and wondering if he would be alright.

I remember that September afternoon when I walked out to pull my sheets off the line before the sun went down. I could feel the autumn creeping back into the air as a cold breeze blew across my face. It just increased my anxiety to think that winter was not that far away. What was there to think about that was good? I wondered.

Julie and Norb had recently split up. I'm not sure what the last straw was, but Julie finally just had enough of Norb's drinking and womanizing, took the kids and went up north to Geneva, Illinois. There were many stories floating around, but I didn't pay much attention to them, and I certainly would not want to spread them. Julie was not only my favorite cousin, but my sister as well. I wanted only happiness for her. I was sorry to think that her dreams hadn't worked out as she had planned and her fairy tale life was not the fantasy that I had always imagined it to be.

Sam had taken the kids down to Norbert's store after dinner. He could sense the tension growing in me and decided to give me a break. It was also a chance to cheer up his brother. Norb was lonely these days without Julie. He drank even more now that she was gone. We tried to keep a close eye on him and to make sure he was eating right.

I missed Julie too. We had written to each other a few times, so I knew that she had found a job in Geneva at a mental hospital. I guessed she was happy. I don't know. Everything had changed, since she left. I couldn't blame her for leaving, but it had definitely changed us all. For me, it was just another hole in my life.

I hadn't heard from Jack in several months and I was really worried. The war had ended and our boys were coming home little by little. I kept telling myself that was the reason why I hadn't heard anything from him. He was probably making his way back to us and hadn't the time to write. Another part of me dreaded that I may never see him again. Every time I saw a service man coming down the road, my heart leapt a little, and I'd pray he wasn't coming to give me bad news. I'd relax a bit when I saw it was someone I knew just returning home to his family. He'd smile and tip his hat to me and I would smile back. "Welcome home!" I would shout to him, wishing that the next one on the road would be Jack.

One by one, I pulled the clothespins down and folded the sheets into a laundry basket. The sun was falling quickly now. As each sheet came down, I came closer and closer to the blinding orange light that was awaiting me on the other side of my clothesline. I pulled down the corner of the last sheet and the golden beams shot right at me like a photographer's flash and I was semi-blinded. Across the road was Zion cemetery in my direct line of sight. The setting sun's pinks and oranges were dancing playfully along the tops of the headstones.

Just for a second I thought I saw a figure among the lights and shadows. I blinked several times to clear some of the flashes from my sight. Yes, there was a figure. It was coming toward me. As it moved closer, I made out a soldier's cap on his head. *Another one of our boys coming home,* I thought to myself. *Another mother will sleep peacefully tonight.* I wished that mother could be me. I continued to pull the last sheet off the line and place it in my basket.

Out of the corner of my eye, I could see that this soldier was not passing by as so many others had. He was definitely headed straight for me, so I put down my laundry basket to see more clearly. I rubbed my eyes and blinked. Suddenly the figure came into focus and I gasped. My heart began to pound. I raised my hand to my open mouth expecting sound to come from it, but nothing would.

Tears rushed to my eyes as I recognized the soldier crossing the road. It was Jack! I ran to him and met him halfway across the gravel road. Jack picked me up in his arms, while I wrapped mine around his neck. No words were spoken. I just held onto him as tightly as I could. Through my tears I saw the sun drop down and out of sight. Still we stood there in the cool darkness holding onto one another. My boy was home! I could breathe again.

Chapter 14

The next page of the album held pictures of Ellie. I imagine it was hard to grow up the only girl in a family so dominated by boys but she was able to hold her own. I watched her grow into a young woman in these pictures. There was a picture of her when she graduated high school and next to it a picture of her wedding day. Ellie married a good man and raised three children. For a long time she lived just a few blocks from Jack in Waukegan.

Photos of Curtis appeared on the next page. Curtis may have been the most handsome son that Sam and I had, but oh what a temper he had! I guess that came from the Reeves' side.

Curtis was always in a fight with someone. Like his uncles, he had a heart of gold, but a hot streak that ran through him that no one—not even he—could control. Still, he managed to grow up and make us proud. He married a young woman from Texas where they settled with their three children.

The years flew by. The children grew up. Sam and I got old. Well, we thought we were old. Being 96 and looking back, 64 doesn't sound so old. Most of Sam's red hair had fallen out and what was left had turned gray. My hair was mostly gray too, and I'm sure I looked older than I was, but then I always had. I never wore makeup and I wouldn't dream of coloring my hair. Sam didn't mind. He still looked at me in the same way as he did that rain soaked night in Marion. We were content in our older years, and we enjoyed our time alone together, working in the garden, taking walks, and watching television.

Occasionally our time was interrupted by wonderful visits from our children and our grandchildren, which we enjoyed immensely. We would take turns visiting some of the kids' favorite places such as the Garden of the Gods with the large rock formations that looked like camels or Indian heads. A few times we visited the Old Slave House in Equality, the only place in Illinois where slavery occurred. Sometimes, we would just head off to Bell Smith Springs and enjoy splashing in the cool water and picnicking. Where we went didn't matter so much as we enjoyed the company of our family.

We bought Julie and Norb's 2 story farm house in 1960. After Julie and he split up, Norb went really wild with drinking. One night he rolled his car down the side of a hill on route 13 between Marion and Carrier Mills and was killed. He and Julie were never legally divorced, so when he died she still owned the house and sold it to us. We certainly didn't need the room (except when the children visited) but the garden was large and the view was spectacular from several different vantage points.

From my front porch I could look across the road and onto a field that sloped down into a valley filled with tall prairie grass and wild flowers. Off the kitchen was a large porch that looked out onto our garden. Our vegetable garden was huge. We grew everything— tomatoes, peppers, potatoes, beans, squash, pumpkin, watermelon, and, of course, strawberries. In front of the vegetables were several rows of flowers—sunflowers, roses, peonies, cock's comb. Sam was so proud of it. Beyond the garden was Mr. Peyton's pond. Out my kitchen window I could see for miles, nothing but sky and grass.

I loved that old farmhouse. 5 screen doors led out onto 3 different porches. In the summer, when the grandchildren were here, the sound of squeaking and slamming could be heard nonstop as they ran in and out of the house. It was a beautiful sound. During the cold lonely winter days I could look up from my quilting, close my eyes and imagine the sound of the little rascals running through the house. In one door and out the other, laughing and screaming, banging and squeaking all day long. Those summer sounds kept me warm on those long January evenings.

Sam and I had the bedroom on the first floor. Along with the house, Julie left us her maple four poster bed with matching dressers and –of course—her lovely vanity with the large round mirror and tufted stool! The little cut glass lamps still sat on either side of the mirror, but now my hair pins and perfume bottles adorned the rest of it. I sat there looking into the mirror that had once belonged to a princess and was now mine. Had I truly become the princess I always dreamed of becoming?

After serving in Korea, Jack settled in Waukegan, Illinois where he met his wife, Caroline. He found a good job at the city water plant and they raised four children. Unfortunately, Jack inherited more than beautiful eyes from J.C. and he took to drinking and gambling. This caused quite a strain on their marriage. I was spared the details, but I knew what was happening and I felt for Caroline. After all I had been in her shoes at one time. I knew the pain that she was experiencing and I admired her strength and determination to keep her family together.

In the summer of 1970 Jack, Caroline and the kids came to visit for the July 4th holiday. We spent the day at Burden Falls swimming and picnicking. Their oldest, Jodi, was now 17. Her brother Tim was 15. Dottie was 14 and the youngest, Greg, was 12. I enjoyed watching the kids running across the rocks and jumping into the water, their voices echoing between the bluffs just as mine and Jack's had many years before.

Being July in Southern Illinois, the air was heavy and hot. While the kids played in the water, the adults took their shoes off and waded around to cool off. We enjoyed a nice picnic lunch and then went into Harrisburg later that night to watch some fireworks. It was a very pleasant day, despite the fact that Jack was sneaking off every couple of hours to have a drink. I did my best to act as if I didn't notice and to have a good time for the sake of Caroline and the kids.

They promised to stay through the end of the week, so I figured I would find a more suitable time to talk to them both. I wanted to enjoy the holiday. I also had no idea what I was going to say. I took most of the next day just trying to think of the right words and the right time to say them.

Late in the afternoon of the 6th, I heard the sound of Jack's station wagon start up and back down the drive onto the gravel. I heard Caroline's footsteps head upstairs. My mind tossed around the idea of going up to talk to her, but wondered if I would just come off as a meddling mother-in-law. I stared up the flight of stairs waiting for an answer to come as to what I should do. The sound of Dottie's voice yelling, "Mama!" as she ran up the stairs to Caroline told me that this was not the appropriate time.

I decided to go out to the garden and pick beans. It was a hot muggy July evening, but as the sun began to sink in the sky, it was cooling ever so slightly. As I picked the beans I prayed to God for guidance. Jack was my darling son. It made no difference that he was now a 47 year old man; he would always be my little blonde headed boy. My sweet boy!

God, give me the strength and the words to confront this situation or give me the patience to leave things be and let them play out naturally, I prayed. I picked and I prayed. I thought and I picked. I wasn't sure if it was the heat or the intensity of my thoughts that brought such a sweat to my brow. The moist air hung heavily around my neck and weighed on me as much as my worries.

My bowl was just about full of beans when I heard a car pull up in the drive. I thought it would be Jack returning and decided I should head him off before he got in the house. Maybe we could walk and have a mother-and-son talk. Just in case he had been drinking, it would give the liquor a chance to wear off before he went in to see Caroline.

I set my bowl of beans down at the edge of the garden and started around the front of the house. As I turned the corner, the blazing bright orange light from a spectacular sunset flashed into my eyes. All I could make out was a figure of a man coming toward me. His long tall silhouette against the setting sun was so striking. I smiled as I saw my young Jack returning home from the war in his uniform alive and healthy and marching through the cemetery after escaping death. My smile faded quickly, though, as the figure came closer and revealed it was not Jack at all.

Chapter 15

I wiped the sweat from my forehead and eyes with my sleeve and I looked again into the bright light. It was a police officer. He removed his cap and said, "Good evening, Ms. Reeves. How are you tonight? You probably don't remember me, but I went to school with your son James."

I stared up at him with questioning. "James?" I said.

"Yes, James, but that was a long time ago. I doubt that you'd remember." He could see the questions I had floating in my eyes.

"What brings you out tonight?" I asked. I could feel myself begin to tremble as I contemplated the many possible answers to that question.

"Ma'am, I know you're also Jack Keller's mother. I was wondering if you knew if your son Jack drove a light blue station wagon."

"Yes," I said. I felt a lump rise in my throat. Something was just not right. I asked, "Is Jack in some kind of trouble, officer?" I suddenly felt the guilt of letting him go out driving when he'd probably been drinking. *Why hadn't I stopped him?*

"Well, ma'am is your husband about this evening?" he asked. His eyes turned down a bit in the corners and a touch of nervousness was apparent, where I hadn't noticed before. Beads of sweat ran down his cheek. His hair was soaked and I realized now as I studied his actions that his hands were tightly wringing his cap at his waist.

A feeling came over me next that was so powerful. Suddenly there was heaviness in my body and it was an effort to breathe. An invisible force had taken over me and was pulling me down as if I were drowning. I yelled out "Sam!" as if I were reaching for a lifeline to catch onto before I went under in this unseen pool. "Sam!" I screamed again. "Sam! Sam! Sam!" As I came up for air, I realized he was standing next to me. I held onto him tightly and tore at his shirt as if he could somehow save me.

"Mr. Reeves" the officer went on, "I'm sorry to inform you that we found Jack's car just a few miles off of Route 45 on the Ozark Road. It was overturned on the curve. It appears that the driver was killed instantly. We believe the driver was your son, Jack Keller."

A breathy "No," fell from Sam's mouth.

"Sir, I'm so sorry to have to give you this news. But, Sir, I also need to ask you if you could come down and identify the body this evening."

I went into a maddening blackness at that point. I was shaking all over. I started wailing and screaming, "Not my Jack! Not my Jack! Not my baby!" But no matter how many times I said it, I couldn't change the look that these two men had on their faces.

The screen door slam caused us all to turn our heads as Caroline walked out onto the porch. She didn't say a word. She just stared at us. I turned back to Sam and pulled at his shirt and screamed. "This can't be happening!' I thought. I grabbed tighter at Sam as I felt myself beginning to fall backwards. I was going under and I couldn't hold tight enough to Sam to stop it. I pulled and I screamed, but the darkness overwhelmed me until I was completely submerged. I surrendered.

I woke up to the sound of birds and the warm breeze blowing the soft white sheers from the open bedroom window. The shade was half drawn and it made a slapping sound as the wind blew it into the room and then sucked it up against the screen. I lay there in the state between dreaming and wakening, wondering what was real. *Had it all been a dream?* I wondered. There was only one way to be sure. I couldn't stay in bed any longer. I swung my legs to the floor and tucked my feet into my soft slippers and made my way to the kitchen to find Sam.

Not only did I find Sam, but also James and his wife, Lynn. They were sitting at the kitchen table sipping coffee and all staring at the same invisible spot on the table, as if they were afraid to make eye contact. They looked up as I entered the room, forced smiles, and quickly pulled their eyes back.

It was real. It was not a dream. The funeral was today. *How long had I been asleep?* I was to be dressed and ready by 8:45 to ride to the church with Ellie and her family. I poured myself some coffee, but could only manage a sip before I felt an overwhelming need to vomit.

It was going to be a hot day. It was only 8:30 and it was already in the high 80's. I kept running the warm wet washcloth over my body, but it was no use. I could not cool down and I could not erase the stickiness on my skin. The slamming of car doors told me that the kids were arriving and that I'd better hurry to get dressed.

I didn't ask for this, I kept thinking to myself as I tried desperately to pull my pantyhose up over my damp skin. There was no air conditioning and everything was sweaty. *I had not given my permission to let Jack go,* I thought as I put on my light blue short-sleeved dress that Eleanor had helped me pick out last year for James' wedding. I didn't feel like doing anything with my hair. I brushed it back and sprayed it stiff, and I stuffed my swollen, sweaty, nylon-covered feet into a pair of white pumps. I stood there looking at myself in the round mirror on the vanity. A tired gray-haired old woman stared back at me. Her sad deep set eyes peered through a pair of pearlescent horn-rimmed bifocals. *How did I get here?* I wondered.

Services were held at Olive Church, and then we drove down to the cemetery. I wanted to yell *Stop!* I wanted to make them wait for me to catch up. Wait for me to gain acceptance of this horrible thing before the preacher said his final prayers at Zion. *Maybe there had been a mistake!* They took the flag from the casket and two soldiers folded it in front of me. *Maybe we were rushing through this without making sure this was really Jack that we were burying! Had Sam really gone down to identify the body? How could I be sure?* A soldier came over to Caroline and handed her the flag now neatly folded. *Please, tell me this is all a dream! Tell me my baby isn't really gone!* They didn't stop. They just lowered Jack's casket into the ground. My heart was breaking and, I could not say a word. I continued to go through the motions with everybody else. I thanked them for coming, for their food, for their sympathy, and I kept quiet.

I stayed quiet until all the activities were over and everyone had gone home. I stayed quiet for days until the last screen door had slammed shut. I waited until it was just Sam and I alone again, and it was dark and quiet. We walked out onto the porch together in the moonlight. I looked up at Sam. "Sam, tell me he's not really gone." I could barely get the words out of my mouth before the tears came gushing out of my eyes.

Sam took me in his arms and held me tightly. He stroked my hair and whispered, "Shhh." He kissed my head and stroked my hair some more. It was only then that I felt safe enough to break down and cry like I had never cried before. It was really true. My baby was really gone, and there was nothing I could do except cry.

The world continued to keep turning and life went on as usual. This just made me angry. I could feel myself becoming so bitter, and I didn't like it. But I didn't feel like I had any control over my actions anymore. I was angry with God and angry with the world for letting my son die. Sometimes I would just break down and cry without any warning. Once it started, it was difficult to stop it. I wondered if I would feel this way for the rest of my life. Part of me wanted to go on feeling this way forever, so that I would never forget Jack. Another more rational part of me knew I needed to let him be with God. My husband and my family needed me to be alive for them. Had I forgotten what it was like to live with my father who had eternally mourned for my mother until the day he died? I had to find my way back to living.

I had a dream one night that I was in a darkened room and Jack was standing in the middle of it. There was another figure there, but I couldn't tell who or what it was. It stayed in the shadows. Bright shafts of sunlight broke through tiny slats in the blinds on the windows saving the room from complete darkness. I moved to the center of the room until I was face to face with Jack. All the time I stood there looking at him, this figure lurked around the room. It was impatiently waiting to take Jack away from me. It did not want me to be there, but I continue to have a wordless conversation with my son, despite this figure's feelings toward me. I finally broke the silence and said, "I don't want you to go." Jack looked down at me with his hands on my arms, "I don't want to go either," he said. He hugged me and I held him tightly until it was morning again.

Chapter 16

In 1976 I was 70 years old. Sam was 79. Our son Curtis was growing concerned about us living out in the country at our ages without any help nearby. The little store on the corner was closed down and the nearest grocery store was 30 miles away, the hospital was even further and we didn't own or know how to drive a car. We agreed that it would be safer for us and less troublesome for our kids if we moved into town.

We purchased a small 5 room house in Carrier Mills. Though the house was small, it sat on a large corner lot that backed up to a wooded pond. We had plenty of room for Sam to start a new garden and it was only a few short blocks walk to the grocery store and the bank. We now had modern conveniences we'd never had, like a washer and dryer, running water, central heating, and best of all—an indoor toilet!

Fortunately for us, we moved out when we did. About 6 months after we were gone from the farmhouse, it burned down to the ground. They claimed it was faulty electrical wiring that caused it. That house had afforded us so many happy memories. It was sad to know that it would never stand again on that beautiful spot in the country.

The years were passing more quickly it seemed. Our grandchildren were growing up and becoming young adults. They no longer visited us for the holidays. We took turns going to their houses. It was more convenient that way. The kids had busy lives and it was difficult for them to leave work. Sam and I had all the time in the world and no place to go.

Life had changed considerably for us, but we were making the most of it. We still had a good sized strawberry patch, grew tomatoes, peppers and beans. It was just enough for us to handle. I liked to crochet and quilt and Sam enjoyed his gardening and watching game shows on television. It was entertaining just to watch him watch them.

Of course, even bigger changes lay ahead of us. In the winter of 1982 Sam was diagnosed with cancer. The doctors did not feel that he was strong enough to withstand surgery, so they kept him as comfortable as they could.

I watched my strong handsome husband deteriorate and become so weak that you would not have even recognized him. The cancer ate away at his muscle tissue until there was nothing left but bone. His spirits remained good through the entire ordeal. Sam was a rock to the very end. We knew it was coming, but we just kept carrying on with our normal days and getting the most from the moments we had left together.

For the first time in our lifetime, there was no garden that summer. Sam watched in frustration as grass poked through the unturned earth in our back yard. I would catch him staring out the window at the field behind the house, his eyes filling with tears. It broke my heart to see him so sad, so powerless. He was restless to have a project but didn't have the ability to stay focused on any one thing, so he wandered around the house and yard all day long until he'd wear himself out enough to sleep.

Eventually it became too difficult for him to walk and he could barely speak. He was in bed all the time and I could tell that he was annoyed with his confinement. His mind was still so alert, but his body would no longer cooperate. It was very difficult for me also to see him in such a state of aggravation. I prayed that peace would come to him soon.

It was October, just a few days before Sam's 87th birthday when I turned out the light, rolled over in bed and said "Goodnight, Sam. I love you." I stroked his precious bald head and gave him a tender little kiss. In a thin raspy voice, Sam said, "I love you, too." Then he died.

Sam and I had a wonderful life together. It may not have always been perfect, but having him with me made it that much easier. I couldn't have asked for a better partner to navigate life's bumpy ride with me. But like so many of God's most precious blessings, he drifted in and then drifted back out of my life leaving me to walk the road again alone.

It had been so long since I'd made a decision just for myself. It was like starting all over again. I embraced life's newest challenge with less fervor than I had in the past. I was tired. I reached out to my church and neighborhood activities to keep me busy, but it was hard to ignore the holes that were becoming larger in my existence.

Chapter 17

Ellie and my granddaughter came by in the morning to visit. I didn't feel much like visiting though. I was tired and lying in bed just made me more tired. The doctors said that my skin grafts were healing nicely and I should be able to go home soon. I was looking forward to going home and being with people and things that were familiar to me. It was very frustrating to be cooped up in this room with little to do and no one to talk to at any length.

My granddaughter brought a cassette tape for me that had spiritual songs on it. After she left, the nurse played the tape for me on the little cassette player in my hospital room.

The song began, "Oh Lord, my God, when I in awesome wonder, consider all the worlds Thy hands have made..." It made me think of Curtis' funeral.

Curtis had been grossly overweight in his adult years. He had a massive heart attack in his front yard one day and died. My eyes welled up with tears as the song played on. We'd sung that song so many times over the years—not just at funerals, but our annual Memorial Day gatherings also. Still, I couldn't hear it without crying.

It was Memorial Day weekend 1998, and we were gathered at the cemetery to pay tribute to our family members gone before us and to raise funds for the upkeep. This was a sacred place for us. Many generations of my family and Sam's were buried here. Sam's especially. His went back as far as the Civil War.

I sat on the old church pew near a window. The seat was so hard. The wood was old and was beginning to split right down the center of the pew. If you weren't careful, you could get quite a pinch sitting on that split. The wood was coated with years and years of paint. This year's color was white. The white was refreshing and clean against the blue walls of the church. *Someone must have really liked blue*, I thought to myself as I looked around at the painted blue walls, painted blue ceiling and blue plush carpet.

The piano player was plunking out, "Then sings my soul my Savior, God, to Thee, how great Thou art..." We were all singing aloud. This was part of the annual ritual here.

I looked around at my daughter, Ellie, and son, James, my grandchildren and great-grandchildren that had come in to be here with me. Every year the crowd seemed to get smaller. The grandchildren were mostly grown now and had busy lives. I understood, but it made me sad to see this tradition slowly dying. The importance of these gatherings is to remember and to keep memories alive. How long before the desire to keep them alive would wither and then die? How long before it was forgotten that Sam had been the one to mow and trim the cemetery? He had cared for it as if it was his own. Rows and rows of perfectly lined up trees stood as far as you could see outside this window—a result of Sam's diligence and hard work. I was proud of the roots we had established in this community. I was proud for my grandchildren and great-grandchildren to know where they came from and I prayed that they would continue to pass those stories along.

At meeting's end, we were dismissed. I walked outside into the hot steamy afternoon. I turned to my left and moved my sensible black orthopedic shoes down the gravel path that wound through the cemetery. I paused at Curtis's gravesite. My second-born son rested between two of Sam's brothers. I walked forward and passed my infant brothers' graves on the right. A tall cedar tree stood between the two headstones. My father planted that tree many years ago. I frowned and shook my head at the lack of foresight my father had. That tree had rooted itself deep into the graves and was making such a mess of the headstones. Next to my brothers were my mother and father. Next to them lay my sister, Katie, and brother, Charles.

Down the path a little further I came to a stop at Jack's grave. I looked up from this spot and gazed across the road to see the little white house where we once lived. I realized that Jack must have been standing right about here whenever I saw him that day returning home from the war. Just for a moment I could see myself in my printed cotton dress running across the field with my arms opened wide to welcome my son back from the war. A tear flowed down my wrinkled cheek, and I quickly pulled a tissue from my purse to wipe it away and to blow my nose.

My sweet first-born son lay next to the only father he had ever known—Sam. Sam's grave was marked with a double headstone that bore both of our names. Ellie and I had carefully placed some yellow silk roses in the vases of Sam's headstone the day before and we thought they had looked so cheery. But they paled, understandably, next to the rosy pink flowers in the vases of the head stone next to his. Even in death, Julie's beauty could not be outdone. The body of my dear sweet cousin and sister-in-law lay right next to Sam's and Norbert's.

It is such a strange feeling to get old. How sad and how wonderful at the same time! I thought of how many wonderful stories I had been a part of in this life and how many incredible people I had known and loved. I had the gift of a strong healthy body and mind. I was able to see my children and their children and their children's children grow and become a part of this amazing life. But the shadow side of a long life is saying goodbye to loved ones as they take the journey before you. I'd said farewell to my children, my husband, sister, brother, parents, and countless other family members and close friends.

I lifted my face into the sunshine and felt a slight breeze blow across my forehead. It cooled the beads of sweat that were forming from the May heat. I wondered how many of these days were left for me. How many more loved ones would I lose before it was my time? I loved my children and my grandchildren. I loved my life, but I was growing tired. I was growing weary of the game. I just didn't feel like playing so much anymore.

The silence at the end of the tape brought me back to the present. My eyes were filled with tears. The nurse came into the room and asked me if I was alright. I just nodded and smiled. *Just a lonely old woman half out of her mind,* is what I'm sure the nurse thought. I didn't mind to let her think that. I *was* a lonely old woman, but I was not half out of my mind. I was completely *in* my mind.

I looked down at my body that had once been so strong and now was tired and old. My skin was once creamy white and now it was covered in freckles and spots. Like a vehicle, this body had taken me far on my journey and helped me to experience much of life, but the bumps in the road, the harsh storms, and the force of gravity had taken their toll. No, I was completely *in* my mind. It was my body that had become very little use for me.

Chapter 18

I dreamed I was on a train. Everything was in black and white like an old movie. I could see the train passing along the tracks into a dark fog, and then I realized I was actually on it. I started at the back of the passenger car and made my way to the front. As I walked up the aisle I noticed friends of mine and family members in the seats. I saw my sister, Katie, and my brother, Charles. They smiled at me and I smiled back as I continued walking. I passed by my father and my mother. My mother looked so beautiful and happy! She was exactly as I remembered her—young and beautiful, holding hands with my father. It had been so long since I'd seen my father smile at me. It gave me such peace.

When I reached the front of the car, I turned to look back at them all. I saw my son Curtis and Sam sitting in the front row. No words passed between us. Only our eyes spoke to each other in recognition.

My eyes traveled to the very back of the car where a man sat dressed in a uniform. I walked back a few steps to see him more clearly. The man stood up and took off his cap. It was Jack! I recognized him and I wanted to run to him, but I couldn't. He smiled at me and opened the back door of the car. The brightest light I'd ever seen came flooding in from outside the car. Jack put his cap back on, tipped it to me and then walked through the door. I watched him until he completely disappeared into the light.

I woke up this morning with renewed strength. It was as if I received a shot of energy overnight. My world seemed more vivid. My head was clear. Colors seemed brighter. And my appetite was back! For breakfast, I had coffee, juice, an English muffin with jam, and two strips of bacon.

The doctors came in after breakfast to tell me that I had made good progress and they were moving me to another wing of the hospital. That was welcome news. I had been in the burn unit for 2-1/2 weeks now, and the change of scenery sounded good. I was hoping to get home soon. Spring was just around the corner and there were so many things to do.

I had not been out of bed in all that time except for very short periods. It seemed like it took forever to get my body out of bed. The nurse helped put my feet into some soft white slippers. They helped cushion the blow of the hard floor as I walked to a wheelchair waiting just inside the door. Once in the wheelchair, I was on my way to the next destination.

It occurred to me that life is constantly a series of little trips to new destinations on so many different levels too. There are the many physical places that are stopovers as we make our way, but there are also the abstract places that we visit, such as age or our positions in life. In my lifetime I had visited many places, many ages, and I had been many things to many different people. I had been someone's child and moved on to be someone's mother. I had been someone's friend, lover, sister, and wife. Each station had been very enjoyable for me. Each place I had been, I had tried my best to live fully and presently and when it was time to bid farewell, I did so with an accepting heart. For the past 17 days this little room had been my world. Now these rubber wheels were taking me to the next stop, moving me into unfamiliar territory once again. I curled up my toes inside my slippers to feel the soft terry cloth beneath them as I anticipated my next destination.

My new room was a basic hospital room, but at least it had some color to it. The walls were painted a dusty rose and there were actually a couple of pictures hanging on them. From my bed, I had a view outside of some leafless trees, and my window was framed by a set of brown and rose plaid curtains. It would be pleasant enough to stay here for a few more days before going home.

Ellie and her husband showed up in time to share some dinner with me. Tonight they wheeled me into a lounge area where the three of us could eat together at a table. It was good to be feeling a little like my old self again.

I don't think I had shared a meal with my daughter and her family since last November when I was in St. Louis for my birthday. I turned 96. We were all gathered at the dining room table—my daughter and her husband, their two daughters and their husbands, and of course my dear great grandson. Somebody asked me that night if I thought I would make it to 100. I remember thinking that I wasn't sure I wanted to.

We ate and talked and laughed over dinner. We discussed the future and speculated how long I would be in this room before I could become mobile enough to go home. My home was such a lonely place now. But it was familiar to me. The familiar is very comforting when you're old. I was looking forward to being comfortable again.

The evening passed rather quickly and I grew tired. I guess I had overdone it in all my excitement of newly found energy. This had been a great day! But now all I could think of was closing my eyes and resting. I told my daughter that I was ready to go lie down, so she went to find a nurse to help me into bed.

For some reason the bed felt unbelievably soft. I think I actually heard my tired old bones sigh as they lay down. I lay my head back on the pillow and looked up at Ellie, who was holding my hand. I looked at her hand and thought about how many times I had held it when she was a child to walk with her down the road. I taught these hands how to sew and to make a pie. This was the hand of my little girl who was now a grandmother. I looked into her eyes and I saw a bit of anxiety. She was realizing that she too was on the road to a new destination in life—the one where she let go of her mother and take over the position of the eldest family member. I looked up at her as I did when I was saying goodbye to Jack that day at the train station. I smiled at her and gave her that same *I'm so proud of you* look. Although it had been so much fun, my eyelids insisted on closing. As they fell shut, I saw the tears begin to build in Ellie's eyes. *Now why was she so sad?* We had just had a beautiful evening, and it was just going to get better. I could feel it.

My eyes are closed now, but I don't see darkness. I see only a single light. As the light gets closer, I open my mouth and I take in the air. As I breathe my first breath of Heaven, I feel a new joy like I've never known before and yet feel strangely familiar with at the same time. There are no shoes on my feet now and what I feel beneath them is indescribable. I take my first steps of this new life. What is next, I don't know, but I do know that I am part of something greater. I can feel it and it fills me with great peace. *'Tis grace has brought me safe thus far and grace will lead me home.*

For just a moment, I look back to see where I've been. I can't see people or places, but the memories! The memories are coming with me. How wonderful it was! I am bringing them all with me on this new journey. I take with me the love I have given, the love I have received, the ups and downs of a life filled with joys and sorrows, and I am so thankful that these things are mine. I am so thankful for the opportunity to know so much happiness and pain, excitement and suffering that only comes from loving so deeply and living so fully. I am thankful for the chance I had to walk in this life and how lucky I was to take all those steps in Virginia's shoes.

www.ingramcontent.com/pod-product-compliance
Lightning Source LLC
Chambersburg PA
CBHW071946170626
46813CB00005B/1842